'Dancing in my nuddy-pants!'

You'll laugh your knickers off!

The Confessions of Georgia Nicolson:

Angus, thongs and full-frontal snogging

'It's OK, I'm wearing really big knickers!'

'Knocked out by my nunga-nungas.'

'Dancing in my nuddy-pants!'

'...and that's when it fell off in my hand.'

'...then he ate my boy entrancers.'

'...startled by his fury shorts!'

'Luuurve is a many trousered thing...'

Also available on tape and CD:

'...and that's when it fell off in my hand.'

'...then he ate my boy entrancers.'

'...startled by his fury shorts!'

'Luuurve is a many trousered thing...'

'Dancing in my nuddy-pants!' ♥

You'll laugh your knickers off!

Louise Rennison ♥

HarperCollins *Children's Books*

This edition produced for The Book People Ltd,
Hall Wood Avenue, Haydock, St Helens, WA11 9UL

Find out more about Georgia at www.georgianicolson.com

First published in Great Britain by Piccadilly Press Ltd 2002
Published by Scholastic Ltd 2003
This edition published by HarperCollins *Children's Books* 2006
HarperCollins *Children's Books* is a division of HarperCollins*Publishers* Ltd,
77-85 Fulham Palace Road, Hammersmith, London W6 8JB

The HarperCollins *Children's Books* website address is
www.harpercollinschildrensbooks.co.uk

1

ISBN 978-0-00-782482-3

Printed and bound in England by
Clays Ltd, St Ives plc

Mixed Sources
Product group from well-managed
forests and other controlled sources
www.fsc.org Cert no. SW-COC-1806
© 1996 Forest Stewardship Council
FSC

FSC is a non-profit international organisation established to promote the
responsible management of the world's forests. Products carrying the FSC
label are independently certified to assure consumers that they come
from forests that are managed to meet the social, economic and
ecological needs of present and future generations.

Find out more about HarperCollins and the environment at
www.harpercollins.co.uk/green

Once again, this work of geniosity is dedicated to my lovely family (whom I lobe very much) and my beyond marvy mates. To Mutti, Vati, Soshie, John, Eduardo Delfonso Delgardo, Honor, Libbs, Millie, Arrow and Jolly, Kimbo, the Kiwi-a-gogo branch, Salty Dog, Jools and the Mogul, Big Fat Bob, Jimjams, Elton, Jeddbox, Lozzer, Mrs H, Geoff, Mizz Morgan, Alan "it's not a perm" Davies, Jenks the Pen, Kim and Sandy, Black Dog, Downietrousers and his lovely fiancée, Andy Pandy, Phil and Ruth, Cock of the North and family, Lukey and Sue, Tony the Frock, Ian the Computer, the Ace Gang from Parklands, St Nicks.

To the English team: Brenda, Yasemin (hi!!!), Margot and everyone at Piccadilly. An especial thank you to the marvellous Emma, the best press person known to humanity.

To the gorgey Scholastic types: David, Gavin, Jessica and Helen.

Much love and thanks to the fabulous Clare (the Empress) and to Gillon, as always.

Thank you to the HarperCollins family.

And finally, *Dancing in my nuddy-pants* is dedicated to the lovely people who have read my books and written to tell me how much they *aime* them.

I love you all.

I do.

Honestly.

She who laughs last laughs the laughingest

Sunday November 21st
My bedroom
Midday as the crow flies
Throwing it down

I've just seen a sparrow be quite literally washed off its perch on a tree. It should have had its umbrella up. But even if it had had its umbrella up it might have slipped on a bit of wet leaf and crashed into a passing squirrel. That is what life is like. Well it's what my life is like.

Once more I am beyond the Valley of the Confused and treading lightly in the Universe of the Huge Red Bottom. What is the matter with me? I love the Sex God and he is my only one and only, but try telling that to my lips. Dave the

Laugh only has to say, "You owe me a snog," and they start puckering up. Well, they can go out on their own in future.

12:30 p.m.

I wonder why the Sex God hasn't phoned me? The Stiff Dylans got back yesterday from their recording shenanigan. Maybe he got van lag from travelling from London? Or maybe he has spoken to Tom and Tom has just happened to say, "Oh Robbie, we all went to a fish party last night and when we were playing Truth, Dare, Kiss or Promise your new girlfriend Georgia accidentally snogged Dave the Laugh. You should have been there, it was a brilliant display of red bottomosity. You would have loved it!"

Oh God. Oh Goddy God God. I am a red-bottomed minx.

12:35 p.m.

On the other foot, no one saw me accidentally snog Dave the Laugh, so maybe it can be a secret that I will never tell. Even in my grave.

12:45 p.m.

But what if Jas has accidentally thought about something

else besides her fringe and put two and two together *vis-à-vis* Dave the Laugh, and blabbed to her so-called boyfriend Tom.

She is, after all, Radio Jas.

1:00 p.m.

I would phone Jas but I am avoiding going downstairs because it's sheer bonkerosity down there. Mr and Mrs Across the Road have been over at least a trillion times saying, "Why? Oh why???" and, "How?" and occasionally, "I ask you, *why*? And *how*?"

At least I am not the only red-bottomed minx in the universe, or even in our street, actually. Naomi, their pedigree sex kitten is pregnant, even though she has been under house arrest for ages. Well, as I have pointed out to anyone who can understand the simplest thing (i.e. me and... er... that's it), Angus cannot be blamed this time. He is merely an innocent stander-by in furry trousers.

2:05 p.m.

I was forced to go downstairs in the end to see if I could find a bit of old Weetabix to eat. Fortunately Mr and Mrs Across the Road had gone home. However, the Loonleader (Dad) was huffing and puffing about trying to be grown-up, twirling his ridiculous beard and adjusting his trousers and so on.

I said, "Vati, people might take you more seriously if you didn't have a tiny badger living on the end of your chin."

I said it in a light-hearted and *trés amusant* way, but as usual he went sensationally ballistic. He shouted, "if you can't be sensible, BE QUIET!"

Honestly, the amount of times I am told to be quiet I might as well have not wasted my time learning to speak.

I could have been a mime artist.

2:15 p.m.
I mimed wanting to borrow a fiver but Mutti pretended she didn't know what I wanted.

Back in my bedroom
2:45 p.m.
Mr and Mrs Across the Road came around again with the back-up loons (Mr and Mrs Next Door). I thought I had better sneak down and see what was going on. No sign of

Angus, thank the Lord. I don't think this is his sort of party (i.e. a cat-lynching party).

Mr Across the Road (Colin) is a bit like Vati, all shouty and trousery and unreasonable. He said, "Look, she's definitely, you know, in the… er, family way. The question is, who is the father?"

Dad (the well-known cat molester) said, "Well, Colin, as you know, we took Angus to the vet and had him… er, seen to. So there is no question in that department."

Mr Across the Road said, "And they were… dealt with, were they? His… well… I mean they were quite clearly… er, snipped?"

This was disgusting! They were talking about Angus's trouser-snake addendums, which should remain in the privacy of his trousers. They rambled on for ages, but as Gorgey Henri, our French student teacher, would say, it is "*le grand mystère de les pantaloons*".

Which reminds me, I should do some French homework so that I stay top girl in French.

2:55 p.m.
This is my froggy homework: "Unfortunately while staying

in a *gîte*, you discover that your bicycle has been stolen. You decide to put an advert in the local paper. In French, write what your advert would say."

3:00 p.m.

My advert reads, "*Merci beaucoup.*"

3:00 p.m.

I cheered up a bit because Grandad came round and set fire to himself with his pipe. He didn't put it out properly and then put it in his trouser pocket. It was only my quick thinking with the soda siphon that prevented an elderly inferno.

4:05 p.m.

Still no call from SG. I am once more on the rack of love.

4:10 p.m.

Phoned Jas.

"Jas."

"What?"

"Why did you say 'what' like that?"

"Like what?"

"You know sort of… funny."

"I always say 'what' like that, unless I'm speaking French; then I say '*quoi*?' or if it's German I say…"

"Jas, be quiet."

"What?"

"Don't start again, let me get to my nub."

"Oo-er."

"Jas."

"Sorry, go on then, get to your nub."

"Well, you know when we were playing Truth, Dare, Kiss or Promise…"

She started laughing in an unusually annoying way, even for her – sort of snorting. Eventually she said, "It was a laugh, wasn't it? Well, apart from when you made me put all those vegetables down my knickers. There's still some soil in them."

"Jas, now, or any other time is not the time to discuss your knickers. This is a situation of sheer desperadoes, possibly."

"Why?"

"Well, I haven't heard from the Sex God and I thought maybe…"

"Oh, didn't I tell you last night? He told me to tell you to meet him by the clock tower. He has to help his olds unpack some stuff for the shop this afternoon. Apparently they are going to sell an exciting range of Mediterranean vine tomatoes that–"

"Jas, Jas. You are obsessed by tomatoes, that is the sadnosity of your life, but what I want to know is this: WHAT TIME did Robbie say to meet him at the clock tower???"

She was a bit huffy with me, but said, "Six o'clock."

Oh, thank you, thank you. "Jas, you know I have always loved you."

She got a bit nervous then. "What do you want now? I've got my homework to do and..."

"Jas, Jas my *petite amie* do not *avez-vous une* spaz attack, I'm just saying that you are my number-one and tip-top pal of all time."

"Am I?"

"*Mais oui.*"

"Thanks."

"And what do you want to say to me?"

"Er... goodbye?"

"No, you want to say how much you love me *aussi*."

"Er... yes."

"Yes what?"

"Er... I do."

"Say it, then."

There was a really long silence.

"Jas, are you there?"

"Hmm."

"Come on, ours is the love that dares speak its name."

"Do I have to say it?"

"*Oui.*"

"I... love you."

"Thanks. See you later, lezzie." And I put down the phone. I am without a shadow of doubtosity VAIR *amusant*!!!

4:30 p.m.

Just enough time for a beauty mask to discourage any lurking lurkers from rearing their ugly heads, then in with the heated rollers for maximum bounceability hairwise. And finally, a body inspection for any sign of orang-utanness.

4:45 p.m.

Now, then, a few soothing yoga postures to put me in the right frame of mind for snogging. (Although I bet Mr Yoga says, "Avoid headstands while using hair rollers, as this causes pain and crashing into the wardrobe." Only he would say it in Yogese, obviously.)

Uh-oh, I fee a bit of stupid brain coming on. Think calmosity.

5:00 p.m.

Fat chance. I was just doing "down dog" when Libby burst in and started playing the drums on my bottom, singing her latest favourite, "Baa Baa Bag Sheet", that well-known nursery rhyme. About a bag sheet that baas. "Baa Baa Bag Sheet" has replaced "Mary Had a Little Lard Its Teats Was White Azno", which she used to love best.

5:05 p.m.

No sign of Angus. The loons are still having a world summit cat meeting downstairs. I heard clinking from the kitchen, which means that the *vino tinto* is coming out, so there will probably be fisticuffs later when they get drunk.

Usual dithering attack about what to wear. It's officially dark by five o'clock so I need to go from day to evening wear. Also it's a bit nippy noodles.

5:10 p.m.
So I think black polo-neck and leather boots... (and trousers of course). And for that essential hint of sophisticosity I might just have to borrow Mum's Paloma perfume. She won't mind. Unless she finds out, of course, in which case she will kill me.

5:15 p.m.
Mum has got a plastic rainhat in her bag! How sad it would be to see her in it.

Still, on the plus side it means that she is taking a more reasonable attitude towards her age. Hopefully it means that she will be throwing away her short skirts and getting sensible underwear.

Oh, hang on, it's not a rainhat, it's a pair of emergency plastic knick-knacks for Libbs. Fair enough, you can never be too careful *vis-à-vis* emergency botty trouble and my darling sister.

5:30 p.m.

Sex God, here I come!!!

I didn't bother to interrupt the loon party; I just left a note on the telephone table:

Dear M and V,

I hope the cat-lynching party is going well. I have found a bit of old toast for my tea and a Jammy Dodger to avert scurvy and gone out. Remember me when you get a moment.

Your daughter,

Georgia

p.s. Gone to meet Jas about froggy homework back about 9 p.m.

Hahahaha très amusant(ish).

6:00 p.m.

As I came into the main street I could see the Sex God was waiting for me by the clock tower. I ducked into a shop doorway for a bit of basooma adjusting and lip gloss application. Also, I thought I should practise saying something normal so that even if my brain fell out (as it normally does when I see him) my mouth could carry on regardless. I thought a simple approach was best. Something like, "Hi," (pause, and a bit of a sexy smile, lips parted, nostrils not flaring wildly) and then, "Long time no dig."

Cool – a bit on the eccentric side, but with no hint of brain gone on holiday to Cyprus.

I came out of my shop doorway and walked towards him. Then he saw me. Oh heavens to Betsy, Mr Gorgeous has landed.

He said, "Hi Georgia" in his Sex-Goddy voice and I said, "Hi Dig."

Dig???

He laughed. "Always a bit of a tricky thing knowing what you are talking about at first, Georgia. This usually makes it better..." And he got hold of my hand and pulled me towards him. Quick visit to Number Four on the snogging scale (kiss lasting three minutes without a breath). Yummy scrumboes and marvelloso. If I could just stay attached to his mouth for ever I would be happy. Dead, obviously, from starvation, but happy. Dead happy. Shut up, shut up!! Brain to mouth, brain to mouth: do not under any circumstances mention being attached to his mouth for ever.

The Sex God looked at me when he stopped his excellent snogging. "Did you miss me?"

"Is the Pope a vicar?" I laughed like a loon at a loon party (i.e. A LOT).

He said, "Er no, he's not."

What are we talking about? I've lost my grip already.

Luckily SG wanted to tell me all about London and The Stiff Dylans. We went and had a cappuccino at Luigi's. As I have said many times, I don't really get cappuccinos. It's the Santa Claus moustache effect I particularly want to avoid. Actually, I have perfected a way of avoiding the foam moustache; what you do is drink the coffee like a hamster. You purse your lips really tightly and then only suck through the middle bit. Imagine you are a hamster having a cup of coffee at Hammy's, the famous hamster coffee shop. Shut up, shut up!!!

The Sex God told me all about an agent-type person offering them a record deal and them staying in this groovy hotel with room service and looking around London.

I said, in between sips of hamster coffee, "Did you see the Changing of the Gourds?"

 20

He said, "Changing of the Gourds?"

Oh no... I had forgotten to unpurse my hamster lips.

"Guards. The changing of the *Guards*."

He really didn't seem to mind that he had a complete idiot for a girlfriend because he leaned over the table and kissed me. In public!!! In the café!! Like in a French film. Everyone was looking. Of course then it meant that I had to nip off to the loos for emergency lip gloss application. It's very hard work being the girlfriend of a Sex God; that is what some people might not know.

We left Luigi's and walked towards my house hand in hand. Thank goodness Robbie is tall enough for me. I don't have to do the orang-utan lolloping along that I had to do with Mark Big Gob. I think that must mean that we are perfect partners, because our arms are the same length.

10:05 p.m.

When we reached the bottom of my street I said to the Sex God that it would be better if he wasn't exposed to my parents because of the Angus fandango.

He asked me what had happened and I said, "Well, in a nutshell, Naomi is pregnant and the finger of shame is pointing towards Angus, even though he is well, you know... not as other men in the trouser addendum department."

When I eventually managed to tear myself away SG gave me a really amazing Number Six with a dash of Six and a quarter (tongues with lip-nibbling). I managed to not fall over and I very nearly waved at him like a normal person when he went home. I like to think I handled the whole incident with sophisticosity.

That is what I like to think.

SG is meeting me on Tuesday after Stalag 14. Hurrah!!!

Everything is going to be fabbity fab fab and also possibly *bon*. For evermore.

10:32 p.m.

Wrong. Vati had his usual outburst of insanity when I let myself in.

"You treat this house like a bloody hotel."

As if. The sanitary inspectors would close the place down if they saw the state of my room. What decent hotel has a toddler pooing in its wardrobes?

Kitchen

Mutti was wearing what I think she imagines is a sexy negligée. I tried to ignore it and said, "What happened at the cat-lynching party?"

"Well, even though Mr and Mrs Across the Road think in principle Angus should be made into a fur handbag, they had to admit that he must be innocent of Naomi's pregnancy."

She seems to think it was all quite funny. But then this is the same woman who, when I asked if she had ever two-timed anyone, said, "Yes, it was great."

Poor Angus is an innocent victim of Naomi's red bottomosity. This is a lesson for me about where blatant and rampant red bottomosity can lead. I have had a lucky escape.

10:45 p.m.

I'm so exhausted by the tension of life that I barely have the energy to cleanse, tone and moisturise, let alone tape down my fringe. I am so looking forward to lying down to rest in my boudoir of love.

11:00 p.m.

Libby has got all her toys in my bed AGAIN! All their heads are lined up on my pillow. And some of her toys are quite literally just heads. I don't know exactly how beheading is going to be useful in her future career but she is bloody good at it.

Libbs popped out from my wardrobe in the nuddy-pants, but wearing A LOT of mum's eyeshadow, and not on her eyes.

"Heggo, Ginger, it's me!!!"

"I know it's you, Libbs – look, sweetheart, wouldn't you like to go in your own snuggly, cosy bed and—"

"Shut up, bad boy. Snuggle."

"Libby, I can't snuggle; you've got too many things in my bed."

"No."

"Yes."

"Get in."

"Look, let me just take something out to make a bit of room... look, I'll just take this old potato—"

"Grr..."

"Don't bite!!!"

Midnight

If I have to sing "Winnie Bag Pool" to Mr Potato one more time I may have to kill myself.

I went to my so-called parents' bedroom door and talked to them from outside in the hall. I've seen Dad in his pyjamas before and it's not a sight for someone as artistic and sensitive as *moi*.

"Hello... it's me. Georgia. Remember Me? Your daughter. And your other daughter, Libby, do you remember her? Two foot six, blonde, senselessly violent?? Ring any bells?"

Vati yelled, "Georgia, what is it now? Why aren't you in bed? You've got school tomorrow."

"Hello, Father, how marvellous to speak with you once again..."

"Georgia, if I have to get out of bed and listen to more rubbish from you... well, you're not too old to smack, you know!"

Smack? Has he finally snapped? He's never smacked anyone in his life. The last time he lost his rag with me, he threw his slipper and it missed me and broke his hilarious (not) mug in the shape of a bottom.

Mutti opened the bedroom door unexpectedly as I was leaning against it and I nearly fell into her basoomas.

She finally persuaded Libby to go into her and Dad's bed. So thankfully Libbs clanked off with Mr Potato, Pantalitzer, Charlie Horse, scuba-diving Barbie and the rest of her "fwends".

I was just snuggling down to go off into boboland when I heard her pitter-pattering back into my room. Oh dear God, she hadn't left something disgusting lurking in the bottom of my bed, had she?

She came right up to me and whispered in my ear, "I lobe you, Ginger. You are my very own big sister."

Awww. I put my hand on her little head. Sometimes I love her so much I feel like I would plunge into a vat of eels to save her. If she fell in one, which in her case is not as unlikely as you might think.

As a lovely goodnight treat, she sucked my ear, which was not pleasant, especially as she was breathing very heavily. It was like a big slug snoring in your ear. Still, very sweet.

Ish.

12:10 a.m.

I've accidentally got to Six and a half on the snogging scale with my little sister.

12:12 a.m.

The Sex God does varying pressure, like Rosie says foreign boys do. Soft, then hard, then soft. Yummy scrumboes.

Oh Robbie, how could I ever have doubted our love?

12:15 a.m.

Dave the Laugh is a bit full of himself, anyway. What was it he said at the fish party? "You have to choose: a Sex God or me, who you can really have a laugh with."

Yes, well, I have chosen. And I have not chosen you, Mr Dave the Laughylaugh. She who laughs last laughs the laughingest.

12:20 a.m.

He has got fantastic lip-nibbling technique, though.

12:25 a.m.

I have gone all feverish now. I wonder where Angus is? I've

not heard any wildlife being slaughtered for ages. Or the Next Doors' poodles Snowy and Whitey (also known as the Prat Brothers) yapping. He must be feeling really depressed. In a cat way.

Haunted by his lost love.

Half the cat he was, and only fading memories of his trouser-snake days.

12:29 a.m.
What is it with my bed? Angus had got a perfectly cosy cat basket, but *oh* no, he has to come in with me.

12:37 a.m.
And why does he like my head so much? It's like having a huge fur hat on.

Why does he do that?

Why?

Monday November 22nd
8:25 a.m.
Everyone late for everything. When Mutti took Libby to kindy, both had hair sticking on end like they had been

electrocuted. They should try the cat hat method – it keeps your hair very flat.

Run, run, pant, pant.

Jas and I panted up the hill to Stalag 14, past the usual assortment of Foxwood lads. They are so weird. Two passed us and started doing impressions of gorillas. Why? Then another group went by, and the biggest one, no stranger to all-over-head acne, said, "Have you got a light?"

Jas said, "No, I don't smoke," and he said, "No chance of a shag, then, I suppose?" And he and his mates went off slapping and shoving each other.

I said to Jas, "They show a distinct lack of maturiosity, but never fear, that is where I come in. I have thought of something *très très amusant* to do with glove animal if it snows this winter."

Jas didn't say anything.

"Jas."

"What?"

"I said something *très amusant* and you *ignorez-voused* me. You do remember good old glove animal, don't you?"

"I know I got three bad conduct marks because you made me wear my gloves pinned over my ears like a big doggy with a beret on top."

"*Voilà*, glove animal. Anyway, I think he should make a comeback this term and liven up the stiffs."

She was pretending not to listen to me but I knew she wanted to really. She was doing fringe fiddling; however, I resisted the temptation to slap her hand, and said, slowly so that she could understand me, "Glove animals have to wear sunglasses when it snows."

"What?"

"Is that all you can say?"

"What?"

"You are doing it to annoy me, *mon petit* pal, but I love you."

"Don't start."

"Anyway, we will have to wear sunglasses with glove animal if it snows, to prevent... snow blindness!!"

She didn't get it, though. I have to keep the comedy levels up at school all by myself.

Assembly
9:20 a.m.

I told the rest of the Ace Gang about the glove animal and snow blindness hilariosity and they gave me the special

Klingon salute. Then I got the ferret-eye from Hawkeye and had to pretend to listen to our large and glorious leader, Slim. Her feet are so fat that you can't actually see any shoe at all. It is only a question of time before she explodes.

Slim was rambling on about the splendour of Shakespeare's *Hamlet* as an allegory for modern times.

For once she is right. Shakespeare is not just some really old boring bloke in tights, because after all it was he who said, "To snog or not to snog, that is the question."

How true, Bill.

Break

Our new pastime to fill in the long hours before we are allowed to go home is called "Let's go down the disco". Anytime any one of the Ace Gang says it, we all have to do manic disco dancing from the 70s (excess head shaking and arm waggling). Even if I do say it myself, it is a piece of resistance.

German

We disco danced at our desks pretty much all the way through German while Herr Kamyer wrote ludicrous things on the board about Herr Koch. As I said to him when we were leaving class, "*Vas is der* point?"

Lunchtime

Very nippy noodles shivering around outside. What harm have we ever done to anyone?

I said that to the gang, "What harm have we ever done to anyone that we are made to go outside in Antarctic conditions?"

Rosie, Ellen, Jools and Mabs all said, "None, we have never done anything."

But Jas, who seems to have turned into Wise Woman of the Forest, said, "Well, there was the locust thing, and the dropping of the blodge lab skeleton on to Mr Attwood's head and..."

Honestly, if I wasn't the girlfriend of a Sex God I would have had to duff Jas up, she is so ludicrously "thoughtful" these days. I think I liked her better when she was all depressed and didn't have a boyfriend. Regular snogging has brought out the worst in her.

The Bummers came by all tarted up. Jackie wears even more make-up than those scary circus people. You know when you go to the circus and you accidentally see a trapeze artist close up and they are orange.

Alison Bummer, unusually spot free, just the one gigantic boil on her neck, shouted over to us as they headed for the back fields and town, "Bye, bye, little girls, have a nice time doing your lessons."

I said, "Honestly, I don't know how they get away with it. They turn up for register, hang around torturing P. Green for a bit, have fifty fags in the loos and then bog off to town at lunchtime, to see their lardy boyfriends."

We had a tutting outbreak as we shared our last snacks.

Rosie was shivering. "It is vair vair nippy noodles. I think I have got frostbite of the bum-oley."

Eventually, in between Nazi patrols led by Wet Lindsay (who may be head girl, but is still: a) wet and b) boyfriendless), we managed to sneak into the science block.

Science block
On our usual radiator
Ellen said, "It was a groovy fish party, wasn't it?"

Rosie said, "*Magnifique*. I found bits of fishfinger everywhere, though. Sven got a bit carried away."

I said, "He should be."

Jas said to Ellen, "What happened at the end? With you and Dave the Laugh, you know, when he walked you home?"

Ellen went all red and girlish. "Oh, you know."

I was prepared to leave it at that, but not old Nosey Knickers. She rambled on. "Did you and Dave the Laugh... do anything?"

Ellen shifted around on the knicker toasting-rack (radiator) and said, "Well..."

I said, "Look, if Ellen wants to have some personal space, well..."

But Ellen was keen as *le moutarde* (keener) to talk about my dumpee. "He did, er, walk me home and..."

The Ace Gang were all agog as two gogs, apart from me. I was ungogged. In fact, I was doing my impression of a cucumber (and no, I do not mean I was lying on some salad... I mean I was being cool).

They all said, "Yes... AND???"

"Well, he, you know, well he, well..."

God's shortie pyjamas, I was going to be a hundred and fifty at this rate.

34

Ellen went red and started playing with her piggies (very annoying) and went on. "It was cool, actually. We got, well, we sort of got to Number Three and a bit."

What is "sort of Number Three and a bit" on the snogging scale? Perhaps I should "sort of" give her a good slapping to make her talk some sense. But no, no, no, why did I care? I was a mirage of glaciosity.

As the bell went for resumption of abnormal cruelty (maths), Ellen said to me, "Dave does this really groovy thing, it's like, er... lip nibbling."

He had nip libbled with her!! The bloody snake in the tight blue jeans had nip libbled her. How dare he??

Ellen was rambling on. "We should add lip nibbling to our snogging scale."

Jas said, "We already have, it's Six and a Quarter."

Ellen said to Jas, "Oh, have you done lip nibbling, then? With Tom?"

Jas went off into the dreamworld that she calls her brain. "No, because Tom really respects me and knows that I want to be a prefect, but Georgia has done it. And she's done ear snogging."

Then they all started. "Is that what the Sex God does?"

"Does it make you go deaf?" and so on. Triple *merde*.

As we went into maths, Ellen said, "You know when we played that game and you were supposed to snog Dave, well... did you?"

I went, "Hahahahahahahahahahaha." Like a hyena in a skirt. And that seemed to satisfy her.

Once again I am in a state of confusiosity. In fact, I can feel my bottom throbbing again when I get a picture of Dave the Laugh nibbling my lips.

And now Ellen's.

He is a serial nip libbler. I am better off without him.

French

Mon Dieu. Fabulosity all round. We are going on a school trip to *le* gay Paree next term. We were yelling, *"Zut alors!"* and *"Mon Dieu!"* and *"Magnifique!!!"* until Madame Slack threw a complete nervy strop. The fabby news is that Gorgey Henri is going to take us. The unfabby news is that Madame Slack and Herr Kamyer, dithering champion for the German nation, are also going. Still, that will be a bit of light relief. Herr Kamyer is almost bound to fall in the Seine at some time over the weekend.

I wrote a note to Rosie: How much do you bet we can do the famous "Taking a souvenir photograph" of Herr Kamyer on the banks of the Seine and he falls in when we say, "Just step back a bit, Herr Kamyer, I haven't quite got your lederhosen in yet."?

4:20 p.m.
Walking home with Jas. I was trying to use her as a windbreak, but she kept dodging away from me. She is unusually full of selfishosity for someone who loves me.

I said, "Thank Cliff Richard's y-fronts that nobody knows about my accidental snogging incident."

"What snogging incident?"

"I can't tell you. It's a secret I'm taking to my grave."

Oh *sacré bleu*. What is the matter with Jas (besides the obvious)?

When I accidentally told her my secret that I will never tell, even in my grave, she went on and on about how I should be ashamed. She is so annoyingly good, like Mother Teresa with a crap fringe.

Home

Mutti in an unusually good mood. She had even bought a pie for us on the way home. Scarily like a real mum – apart from the ludicrously short skirt. She's not going to tell me that I'm going to have another little brother or sister, is she?

Still, I can't think of everyone else. I am not God, I have enough to worry about thinking about myself.

8:00 p.m.

I am so worried about school tomorrow. I have so much to do.

8:10 p.m.

I can do my nails and foundation and eye stuff during RE – Miss Wilson won't notice, as she will be sadly rambling on about the Dalai Lama or yaks or whatever it is she does talk about. But I suppose even she might notice if I took my curling tongs into class. I'll have to do my hair at lunchtime and hope the Bummers don't decide to put their chewing gum in it for a laugh.

Looking out of my bedroom window

I'm amazed to see Naomi the sex kitten lounging around on the roof of our shed, showing off her fat tummy. She has got very little shame to say she is an illegitimate bride. Angus is in the garden below her, blinded by his love. Well, actually he's mostly blinded by the dirt he's digging up. He's got a huge bone from somewhere and he's burying it. Maybe as a midnight snack. He doesn't really seem to understand that he is not a dog. I may have to do some diagrams of mice for him and explain.

I went downstairs to the kitchen to find M and V absolutely all over each other. It's like living in a porn movie living in our house. Honestly, isn't she sick of him yet? (I am.) He's been back about a month; surely by now they must be discussing divorce.

I said, "Erlack," in a caring way to let them know I was there. But my finer feelings make no difference to the elderly snoggers. They just started giggling, like... giggling elderly snoggers.

I said, "Vati, I don't want to be the person responsible for one of your unreasonable outbursts of rage, but..."

He said, "OK, as I am in a good mood you can have a fiver, because you did so well on your French test."

I was quite literally gobsmacked. For a second. Then I grabbed the fiver.

"Er, thanks... but, erm, I feel, in all fairness to you, I should let you know that Naomi is on our shed roof and that Angus is not a million miles away from her. In fact, as I left my room, he was licking her bottom."

No one went ballisticisimus, because apparently Mr and Mrs Across the Road have worked out that the pedigree boy cat they had over to visit with Naomi must have had more than a few fishy snacks with her.

Vati said, "either that or she is having a virgin birth."

Hey, she might be! She might be having a little furry Baby Jesus (lots of them, in fact). She is due to give birth at Christmas, after all. And God works in mysterious ways, as everyone knows.

I said to Jas on the phone, "It makes you think, doesn't it?"

She was all weird and huffy. "No, what makes me think is this: how come some people, naming no names, but you, Georgia, can tell such porkies to their so-called friends?"

She was rambling on about Ellen and Dave the Laugh, of course.

I said with deep meaningosity, "Jas, she who casts the

first stone has to cast the logs out of her own knickers first."

That made her think. Then she said, "What in the name of frankincense are you talking about?"

I had to admit she had me there.

Her trouble is that she has never done anything adventurous, her bottom has never glowed with the red light of... er... red bottomosity.

I said to her, "Jas, Jas, my little nincompoop, I didn't MEAN to snog Dave the Laugh. It was an accident I am a teenager and I can't always control my bits and pieces."

"What bits and pieces?"

"Well, you know, I have very little control over my nunga-nungas, for instance... and at the fish party with Dave my lips just sort of puckered up."

I'm a teenager and I *can* control my bits and pieces."

"What about your fringe?"

"That is not the same as snogging someone else's boyfriend."

"You are getting very set in your ways, Jas."

"I am not."

"Well, name an interesting thing that you and Tom have done lately."

"We've done loads of really interesting, crazy things."

"Like what? And don't tell me about collecting frog spawn."

"Well, Tom is going to do ecology and so on... do you know we found some badger footprints in the park near—"

"Jas, I said name an interesting thing that you and Tom have done lately, not something about badgers."

But she had gone off into the twilight world of her brain. "Tom gave me a love bite."

"*Non.*"

"*Oui.*"

"I've never seen it."

"I know."

"Where is it?"

"On my big toe."

9:00 p.m.

I am worried that in my capacity as the Sex God's girlfriend I may have to give a celebrity interview about my life and Jas will have to come on it. And she will talk rubbish. And perhaps show her love bite. Or pants.

9:15 p.m.

Still, it has taken her mind off the Dave the Laugh fiasco.

I will have an early night to prepare myself for heavy snogging duties. I want to look all gorgey and marvy for SG and not have those weird little piggy eyes that I get sometimes when I have been kept awake all night by loons (Angus and Libby). Mutti has let Libbs sleep in the cat basket with Angus tonight, so I am safe.

9:35 p.m.

Ah... very nice and cosy in bed, although I am having to sleep sitting up because I have rollers in my hair for optimum bounceability.

9:40 p.m.

Phone rang. Vati yelled, "Georgia, another one of your little mates on the phone. You'd better hurry, I think it's an emergency. She might have run out of lip gloss."

Vair vair vair *amusant*, Vati.

As I came down the stairs, he said, "We mean no harm, take us to your leader," because of my hair rollers. He really is in an alarmingly good mood.

♡ 43

It was Ellen. Uh-oh. I hoped she couldn't detect my red minxiness.

"Georgia, can I ask you something?"

"Er, like what?"

"Well, you know Dave the Laugh?"

DID I KNOW DAVE THE LAUGH????!!!!!!

I sounded a bit vague. "I know Dave the woman, but Dave the laugh...? Oh er, Dave the Laugh... yes, what about him?"

"Well, you know I really think he's groovy and so on and he did the lip nibbling thing, and that was, you know, quite groovy and not, you know, ungroovy... and how I have thought he is quite groovy for a long time and lip nibbling would, like, mean he thought I was groovy as well..."

(It was going to be the twenty-second century at this rate by the time she got round to telling me what in the name of Father Christmas's elfin mates Nobby and Les she was on about.)

She was still rambling on for England. "Well, anyway, it's nearly Tuesday."

"Yes and...?"

"Well, he hasn't called me yet," she went on. "Well, what should I do?"

"Did he say he'd call?" (Not that I am remotely interested in what my ex-snogees say. I am just being a great pal.)

"Not exactly."

"What did he say exactly?"

"He said, 'I'm away laughing on a fast camel – see you later.' "

"Oh."

"What?"

"It's the old 'see you later' thing, isn't it?"

"You mean it might be see you later, as in see you *later* not see you later?"

"*Exactamondo.*"

She went on and on about Dave the L and about how surely he wouldn't nip libble her if he didn't like her, etc., etc.... I was so tired I tried to lie down on the floor, but couldn't because of my rollers. Good Lord, what am I? The Oracle of Delphinium?

Eventually she rang off.

10:00 p.m.
What if Ellen finds out about me and Dave the Laugh? Will she still like me and realise that it is just one of those things?

Or will she beat me to within an inch of my life?

How would I feel if the boot was on the other cheek?

I wish I wasn't so caring and empathetic. As Hawkeye said in English, I have a very vivid imagination.

10:15 p.m.

Actually what she said was that I had a "hideous" imagination. But she is just jealous because she has no life to speak of (apart from torturing us).

10:40 p.m.

My nose feels very heavy. I'd better have a look at it in case there is a lurking lurker situation.

10:47 p.m.

Hmm. I can't see anything. It doesn't get any smaller, though. I must make sure I always suck it in when I see the Sex God full on.

10:55 p.m.

On the plus side, my nungas don't seem any more sticky out than they are normally. Perhaps they have stopped growing.

Or maybe they are on Christmas vacation, before they burst (quite literally) into life in spring.

11:00 p.m.
I'll just give them a quick measure.

11:05 p.m.
Sacré bloody *bleu* and also *mon Dieu*!! They measure thirty-eight inches!! That is more than a yard. There must be something wrong with the tape measure.

11:10 p.m.
I've done it again and it's still the same. It amazes me that I can lumber around at all. It's like carrying two small people around with me.

I'm really worried now. I wish there was someone I could talk to about this sort of thing. I know there is an unseen power at work of which we have little comprehension, but I don't really feel I can consult with Jesus about my basoomas.

Or Buddha.

Anyway, I don't want to offend Buddha and so on, just in case He exists, which I am sure He does... but... I have seen some statues of Buddha and frankly his nunga-nungas are not small either.

Midnight

When I was in M&S the other Saturday, I saw a sign that said they had a breast measuring service (top job… not). Maybe I should get properly measured by a basooma professional and learn the truth about my condition(s).

1:00 a.m.

Angus is on the road to recovery. I can hear him serenading the Prat Poodles with a medley of his latest hits: "Yowl!" and "Yowl 2 the remix".

I got up to look. He is so brave in the face of his pain. I really love him, even if he has destroyed half my tights. He could have just given in, but no, there he was, biffing the Prat Brothers like normal. Naomi was parading up and down on the Next Doors' window sill, sticking her bottom in the air and so on. She is an awful minx. She is making a mockery of a sham of her so-called love for Angus. It's like in that old crap song where the bloke is wounded in the Vietnam War and his wife goes off with other men because he can't get out of his wheelchair. He sings, "Ru-beeee, don't take your love to town."

That is what Angus would sing. "Naom-eeeee, don't take your love to town." If he could sing. Or speak. And had a wheelchair.

School panto fiasco (a.k.a. complete twats in tights)

Tuesday November 23rd
Breakfast

Dad was singing, "Sex bomb, sex bomb, I'm a sex bomb," and doing hip thrusts round the kitchen. He'll end up in casualty again if he's not careful. He was being all interested in me as well. Red alert, red alert!

He gave me a hug(!) and said, "I thought we'd all go to the cinema tonight. My treat."

I said "Fantastic!!!" He thought I meant it and went off happily to flood people's homes or whatever it is he does at the Water Board.

I said to Mum, who was trying to get all the porridge out of Libby's hair before she went off to kindergarten, "Mum, I can't go to the cinema tonight, I... I've got to stay behind and help with... the school panto."

She didn't even look up. "I didn't know you were in it."

"I'm not, I'm just, er, helping backstage. Bye, Mutti. Byeeee, Bibbet."

"Bye bye, Gingey, kiss Mr Cheese bye bye."

It was disgusting kissing Mr Cheese. (Mr Cheese is a bit of old Edam in a hat.) Not as disgusting as it will be at the end of the day when Libby brings him home again from playschool. With a bit of luck Mr Cheese will have been eaten by one of Libby's little pals.

I had a look at my pocket mirror as I walked round to Jas's place. Eight out of ten on the hair bounceability front. I am sooo excited. I love the Sex God and it will be beyond fabulosity and into the Valley of Marv when we go on tour to America. I think I could easily write song lyrics myself.

I said that to Jas as we walked to school. "Thank you, ladies and gentlemen, this one is called "Sex God" and it goes like this: 'Oh, Robbie, you're the one for me, with your dark blue eyes and your...'"

I had a bit of writer's block then and I said to Jas, "What rhymes with 'me'?"

"What about 'two-timer'? Or 'crap mate'?"

"Jas, don't start again… oh hang on, I know: 'You're the one for me, with your dark blue eyes and your… snoggability!!!' I am clearly a genius."

I put my arm round Jas in my happinosity and said, "You can show me your love bite when we get to Stalag 14."

She went a bit red and said, "OK, but don't tell anyone else about it." Which is ironic coming from Radio Jas.

Assembly
Slim really on tip-top boring form this morning.

She bored us beyond the Valley of the Dim and into the twilight world of the Elderly Mad.

Speaking of which, we saw Elvis Attwood tapping at pipes with his hammer as we went out.

I said to him, "I think you should receive a knighthood, Mr Attwood, for your services to caretaking. Surely you of all people deserve to be hit over the shoulders with an old sword."

10:00 a.m.
What IS it with this place????!!! Rosie and I have got bad conduct marks AND have to stay behind and help with *Peter*

Pan every night this week after school. I cannot believe it! Just because we have naturally high spirits and *joie de vivre*. (And also got caught doing our "Let's go down the disco" dance to "There is a Green Hill Faraway" in assembly.)

It is so obviously hilarious. And not at all "indicative of stupendous childishness", as Hawkeye said.

10:30 a.m.
Perhaps I am Spawn of the Devil in a skirt and have the third eye. No, I mean the second whatsit... sight. Because I told Mum that I was staying behind to help with Peter Pan, even though I wasn't, and now I am. I may have special powers.

11:00 a.m.
No, I haven't got special powers. I tried for about a million years to make the wall clock fall on to Hawkeye's head, but it just gave me a very bad headache.

In the loos
I said to Jas, "For once in the entire existence of humankind my hair has got bounceability and whatsit and I am on detention."

She said, "Well you shouldn't be so silly."

What is silly about disco dancing?

She wanted to show me her love bite, but I couldn't summon up any interest.

RE

Miss Wilson has written on the board: "Relationships – what are the ingredients?"

Good Lord, she would be the last to know, and also I don't think I have ever seen anyone over the age of six months wearing a pink smock, apart from her. Has she really not got one single mate who would have said to her, "Put the smock in the bin and we will never mention it again"?

I wonder if I should make Naomi a little pregnancy smock. In the spirit of Christmas?

Rosie has made some dreadlocks for her pencil and stuck them on to the end of it. She wrote me a note: As a Rastafarian he has strong views on religious freedom.

I wrote back: It's a pencil, you fool.

And she wrote: That is what makes it even more remarkable.

But we are only trying to cheer ourselves up because of the Peter Pan fiasco.

What am I going to do about the Sex God? He is supposed to meet me after school. I wrote to Jas: If I tell SG I have been given detention duties helping complete twats into tights he will think I am a silly little schoolgirl.

She wrote back: You ARE a silly little schoolgirl.

Cheers, thanks a lot. Goodnight.

Last bell
3:50 p.m.

I ran down the corridor to the cloakrooms and threw myself in front of the mirror. This was my plan: emergency make-up, dash to the school gates, quick snog, explain to Robbie about my unfair incarceration by the Nazis (but not exactly mention the "Let's go down the disco" incident, in case it was construed as a bit on the childish side), another quick snog, possibly Number Four, then quick as a bunny back to the main hall before ten past four.

Pant, pant. *Alors, alors.* Mascara, lippy, lip gloss, rolly-over skirt, bouncey hair, bouncey hair.

Right. Ready for the Sex God in five minutes and thirty seconds. A new world record.

When I stepped out into the corridor, I walked straight into Hawkeye lurking like a piranha. Oh *Scheissenhausen*.

She loomed over me. "Georgia, you are helping with the Christmas entertainment, why does that require mascara? Remove it and go along to the main hall NOW!"

I slunk back in the loos. This called for the famous "Getting out through the loo window and jumping on to the back field" routine. I almost decapitated two first years getting out of the window, but I made it. I ran along the back field and then down Fag-ash Alleyway (so called, because it is where the Bummers hang out) that runs between the science block and... there he was, waiting for me. Sex God unleashed. He looked amazingly groovy. All the girls streaming out of the gates were eyeballing him as they went by. He said hi to Ali King and she practically evaporated on the spot.

After a quick suck in of the nostrils I sauntered out with an attractive air of casualosity and said, "Hi."

Blimey, I'd managed to say something normal to him. That was a turn up for *les livres*. He smiled his smile and said, "Hi."

He put his hand through my hair (feeling its incredible bounceability, probably) and leaned down and kissed me. Wow. I knew that everyone walking past us was looking, but I had my eyes closed. I did try slightly opening my eyes, but I could only see a big sort of blurry pink thing, which gave me a bit of a turn, until I realised it was my nose really close up.

4:15 p.m.

Probably because I am such a kind and caring person, Jesus has decided to take me for His sunbeam by letting me off the hook. The Sex God told me that he had to go and have a "conference call" with some record people from Hamburger-a-gogo land and so he couldn't see me tonight.

I feel a mixture of sadnosity and reliefosity, with just a hint of peckishness.

4:30 p.m.

Rosie and I have the ridiculously sad task of helping the "cast" of *Peter Pan* into their costumes and sorting out the props. We are in charge of the "dressing room", or PE changing room, as the normal might call it. We have to hang everything up in order and on different pegs, while Miss Stamp dashes about "supervising".

Wet Lindsay has got the leading part of Peter in *Peter Pan*, which I think is unfortunate casting, because she has to wear a green tunic and tights. She has got astonishingly stick-like legs. Also, for no good reason (other than I stole her boyfriend), she has taken against me. She wouldn't have me as her little helper, so Rosie has to help her into her tights and so on. (Erlack.) Tragic Kate is Wendy in the show and I have to help her into her duff wig with plaits.

Hours of boredom stretch ahead. Will I never be free of this hellhole?

5:10 p.m.
The SG will be talking to people in Hamburger-a-gogo land now.

6:00 p.m.
I said to Rosie, "Do you and Sven talk a lot?"

Rosie thought a bit. "Sven talks a lot."

"What about?"

"I haven't got the faintest idea. He's not, as you know,

English. Reindeer, possibly."

"Don't you mind that all you do is snog?"

"No."

8:00 p.m.

Home again, in the sanctity of my luuurve boudoir.

Mon Dieu, how boring was the rehearsal? It was almost as boring as Dad's stories about Kiwi-a-gogo land. Still, home at last and my bedroom is a Libby-free zone!

I haven't listened to my dolphin CD for a bit. I think I will put it on and meditate on my inner me.

8:10 p.m.

I don't know who it is that thinks dolphins are soothing. It's just squeak squeaky squeak.

8:15 p.m.

I do feel a bit sorry for them, though, because they get all those depressed people insisting on swimming with them. It might cheer up the depressed people, but I bet it depresses the arse off the dolphins. They just want to go out with their mates for a laugh and no sooner do they start playing Chase the Cod or whatever, than all these miserable types come and hang around stroking their snouts and crying.

Or am I being a bit harsh?

8:35 p.m.
Everyone out as usual, round at Uncle Eddie's. God it's boring being by yourself. I may be forced to do my blodge homework.

9:00 p.m.
Rang Jas.

"Jas."

"*Quoi?*"

"What are you doing?"

"Blodge homework."

"*Moi aussi.* Are you drawing a hydra?"

"*Oui.*"

"Have you drawn its wafting tentacles yet?"

"*Non.*"

"I have. Also I have drawn in some cheesy whatsits being wafted in by its tentacles."

"Hydras don't eat cheesy whatsits. They are pond life."

"That's a bit rude, Jas."

"It isn't – it's a biological fact."

"OK, Jas, but have you considered this? Perhaps hydras don't eat cheesy whatsits because no one has had the GOOD MANNERS to go down to the pond and offer them around! Don't hydras deserve to be treated like human beings?"

9:15 p.m.
Oh, I am so bored!!

In my *Don't Sweat the Small Stuff for Teens* it says: "Do something interesting and useful for others."

9:30 p.m.
I can get forty-eight little plaits in my hair.

9:35 p.m.
It makes me look like a complete twat, though.

9:40 p.m.
Phone rang!!

"Georgia."

Yes and three times yes!!! It was Robbie.

The record company has done a deal with a big American company and they want The Stiff Dylans to go over there on tour and stuff. Wow.

Rang Jas and told her.

"What do you think I should wear to go on tour? You can never go wrong in black, can you?"

"You dad will never in a million trillion years let you go to America on tour with a band."

"You will see, my little pal."

10:00 p.m.

I will miss my Ace Gang when I go off with the Sex God.

Mutti, Vati and Libbs all came home. Libbs said, "Heggo, Gingey," and put her little arms up for me to lift her up. There was the usual wrestling match trying to get her into her own bed but no spitting, thank goodness.

I will really miss her when I go on tour.

10:15 p.m.

I went into the living room to talk to my dear old vati. I feel quite fond of him now I won't be seeing him for much longer. He was lolling on the sofa watching TV, twirling his beard.

"Dad."

"Hmm."

"Er... you know... if I had a really good, life changing experience offered to me well... would you let me go?"

He said, "What fool has offered to adopt you?" And laughed like a bearded loon (which he is).

I went on with great dignity. "Yes, very funny, Dad. Anyway, say I was invited to America – could I go?"

"No."

"Well, could I go to Paris on the school trip, then?"

"I thought you hated Edith Piaf."

"I do, but I *aime* very very much the other French people."

Anyway, the long and the long of it is that I can go on the Paris trip. I gave Dad a little kiss on his cheek when he said yes, and he looked like his head was going to fall off with surprise. But I can be a very kind and caring person, especially if I am about three thousand miles away in a different country.

Midnight

But this is only one string in my mistress plan. First Paris,

France, and then Paris, Texas!!!

Howdy Hamburger-a-gogo types!!

Friday November 26th
French

We've all signed up to go on the French trip to *le* gay Paree, apart from the Bummers (hurrah) and Nauseating P. Green and ADM (Astonishingly Dim Monica). P. Green and ADM are not allowed to go because their mums are worried about the drinking water being polluted in France, and also that they might lose their glasses. Which I think would be a plus.

Gorgey Henri was talking about the trip and sitting on his desk. Phwoar. I know that I am putting my red bottom aside with a firm hand but he is very groovy-looking.

When Gorgey Henri said, "I will show you... how you say... my EVERYTHING in Paris," I said, "Oo-er," which made Rosie laugh uncontrollably for about five minutes.

4:20 p.m.

Forced to stay behind again to help with the *Peter Pan* fiasco. I think it's a crime against humanity to have to look at Wet Lindsay's stick legs night after night. But can I explain that to lesbian of the modern world Miss Stamp? No. She is in a fever of excitement, adjusting costumes, and sending Nana the dog (a.k.a. Pamela Green) scampering around. P. Green is alarmingly good as a dog. I may teach her some amusing tricks.

Backstage
6:00 p.m.

Backstage, rifling through the props box, because Tinkerbell (played by Melanie Griffiths, 48DD in the basooma department) broke her wand when Nana leaped up at her by mistake.

I said to Rosie, as we rummaged around trying to find another one, "Do you think it's awfully wise to let Melanie Andrews loose on stage…?"

Rosie said, "No, I don't. She's not small, is she? What if her enormous basoomas make her topple over and she kills a first former?"

I said, "I think in our capacity of backstage staff we should ban her on health and safety grounds."

Tuesday November 30th

The Stiff Dylans are rehearsing every night. Robbie said I should come along and listen at the weekend when they are doing their new set. I think I should take an interest in my new life. I could make some suggestions about lyrics and so on.

Saturday December 4th

Sven and the lads have organised a nature ramble tomorrow afternoon. I asked Rosie, "What does that mean?"

"Well, you know, we ramble off to the park and then we snog."

I can't go, though, because I am going to go to rehearsal with The Stiff Dylans. They have a "mini-tour" of Scotland and Wales just after Chrimbo. Then they will be cutting their new album. Man. That is not what the album is called. That is just what pop-type people say.

I rang Jas to tell her. "The Stiff Dylans are cutting a new album, man."

"Why is it called 'Man'?"

Sometimes when I talk to Jas I can feel the will to live ebbing away.

Sunday December 5th

Remind me never to go to a band rehearsal again. It is soooooo boring watching other people doing stuff. And talking about themselves. And me not being in it. I just sat at the back and nodded my head for about a million years.

Also, I think the rest of the lads think I'm a bit weird. I don't know why. I have always been the height of sophisticosity around them. Well apart from when Dom, the drummer, asked me what I was going to do at college and I said, "Backing dancing".

Oh and also when I danced around at a gig in front of Dom's dad because I thought he was an American talent spotter, but he wasn't. He was just Dom's dad waiting to help them pack up. And he thought that I was trying to get off with him.

But apart from those two minor hiccups I have been sophisticosity all round, I like to think.

Anyway, here is a brief resume of my glorious night:
- a) nodded my head for a million years
- b) sat on a drum kit in the van on the way home
- c) lost my balance and put my foot through the bass drum

d) had to be dropped off first because I had to be in
    by ten o'clock on a school night

Double *merde*.

At least when I have to do the boring old panto stuff I can have a bit of artistic licence with Rosie.

I wonder how the nature snog went. I suppose Dave the Laugh went with Ellen.

I don't think that The Stiff Dylans think I am full of maturiosity. I think they think I am the Yoko Ono of the band and that I will split them up.

Monday December 6th

I can't believe the poo-osity of my life. Hawkeye said that as "a special treat" Rosie and I could help backstage at the panto again.

Hawkeye is without a doubt a sadist and ex-prison warder. And probably a man.

Panto rehearsals

I taught Nauseating P. Green to catch a mini Mars in her mouth from four foot. She is taking this dog business alarmingly seriously. She even brought me a stick, but as I said to Rosie, "I draw the line at tickling her tummy."

Wet Lindsay was trying to take her tights off by herself when she lost her balance and nearly crashed into the sanitary towel dispenser. It really cheered me up. She got the megahump when I was laughing and doing my impression of her crashing about stuck in a pair of tights. Which was vair vair amusing but old Tiny Forehead didn't think so. After calling me "a pathetic little twit" she stomped off into a cubicle to get changed.

However, as any fool knows, I am the mistress of invention and with the aid of my compact mirror I was able to look under the door of the cubicle. I made Rosie come and have a look in the mirror because she didn't believe that Wet Lindsay wears a thong in real life. But she had to believe the evidence of her own peepers when she saw the thong nestling in Wet Lindsay's bum-oley. Ro Ro had to have a reviving chewy fruit before she could speak again then she said, "I am very sensitive, you know. That sort of thing may ruin my chances of becoming a vet."

So all is well that ends well.

10:00 p.m.

Our house had been a relatively loon-free zone, but it was too good to last. Uncle Eddie was round tonight. As usual, he came balding into my room with one of his hilarious "jokes". He said, "Can a cross-eyed teacher control her pupils?" And looned off laughing like a bald loon.

10:15 p.m.

Robbie phoned and he didn't mention the bass drum incident, which is a plus. He said, "What have you been up to, Sex Kitty?"

Prrrrrrrrrrrrrrr!!!!

Midnight

I do feel like a bit of a French resistance person, though, because I only see Robbie sort of in secret. There is no normal stuff with him. I said that to Rosie and she said, "What do you call normal?"

"Well, you and Sven, you see each other all the time and you must do normal stuff."

She just looked at me. "Have you met Sven?"

Hmmm, she has a point. Jas and Tom do normal stuff,

though. In fact, they act like they have been married for about a trillion years. I'm not saying I want to be as boring as Jas and Tom – collecting frog spawn and doing homework together is too tragic for words. But what do you do with Sex Gods? Besides snog and worship them, I mean.

Thursday December 9th

Opening night of the panto. When the audience started clapping to prove they believed in fairies, Tinkerbell flew out of control and crashed against the back piece of scenery, which fell over to reveal Miss Stamp having a fag. Very funny indeed, I thought.

And much less boring than watching Peter Pan poncing around in green tights.

9:50 p.m.

Something quite alarming happened tonight. I was just sneaking off from the dressing room when Nauseating P. Green came bounding along, still with her dog ears on. And she had her mum, who is not unblessed in the huge glasses department, with her. They were both blinking at me and following me out of the door. Like two giant goldfish in skirts.

P. Green said, "I told Mum that you were the one who really helped me with my dog tricks."

What is the matter with her???

Mrs Nauseating P. Green said, "It's really nice that Pamela and you are such good friends. Would you like to come round to our house on Christmas Eve? We do round robin storytelling and dress up."

I said, "Hrrmmmmm... Oh, is that the time, I must dash!" And made a desperate bid for freedom.

As we walked home, Rosie said, "She loves you very very much. You are her bestest pal." Good grief.

Friday December 10th

Christmas frenzy mounting. I put some tinsel around my sports knickers for that little festive touch in PE. Miss Stamp for once did not have a nervy spaz, which was a bit scary. Things soon got back to normal in Latin, though, because Hawkeye made us take the false snow (cotton wool) off our heads.

Wednesday December 15th
Last day of term
Hurrah!!! Thank you, thank you, Baby Jesus!!! Free, free at last!

Last German lesson
We were all a bit on the hysterical side. I think the teachers must have been out for a pre-Christmas beverage, if you know what I mean, because Herr Kamyer told us an incomprehensible joke about a Swiss cheese (please don't even ask) and then laughed for about forty years. AND as we were going down the corridor we bumped into Gorgey Henri.

"Merry *Noël*," I said to him and he kissed my cheek and said, "*Merci, au revoir.* I look forward to 'aving you all again in the New Year."

Which made us apoplectic with laughter. I thought I might have to throw a bucket of cold water over Rosie and Jools.

Henri smiled at us and said, "You are so crazee." Then he walked off in his groovy gravy jeans.

"Gorgey Henri is quite literally... gorgey," I said. "He is yummy scrumboes and also..."

Rosie said, "Scrummy yumboes?"

"*Mais oui.*"

6:30 p.m.

Last night of the panto. *Mucho excitemondo* (not).

Miss Stamp bought Coca-Cola and cakes for the cast as an end-of-show party thing. Unfortunately the little cakes were saying, "Eat me, eat me, you know you want to," and so Rosie and I were enticed by them. We only ate a few, but Hawkeye noticed and now we are banned from the party. *Quel dommage* (not).

8:00 p.m.

Peter and the rest of the ridiculous Lost Boys are poncing around on stage. I may have to eat myself soon, I am so bored. I wonder where the Sex God is now? And if he is thinking about me. I wonder if he thinks about me as many times a minute as I think about him.

I've had to pretend that I am in training for hockey every night this week. Somehow, even though I believe that the only good relationship is an open and honest one, I can't bring myself to tell him that I am helping people into tights.

8:10 p.m.

Rosie found something *très très magnifique* in a props basket at the back of the store cupboard – theatrical fur. Fake fur that you stick on with a special glue and you can make beards and sideburns and so on with it.

8:25 p.m.

Rosie and I have to be on duty at the side of the stage, handing things over to Wendy and Peter and Captain Hook and so on when they come off. They are all sooo excited. And theatrical. Wet Lindsay just shouts orders like "Sword!" or "Panstick!" if she has to have her stupid shiny forehead touched up. It's VERY annoying, and boring beyond even the Valley of Boredom.

But now we have introduced the theatrical fur into the proceedings. Every time one of us has to go and get something from backstage we stick on a bit of theatrical fur, but just carry on doing our tasks as normal.

8:45 p.m.

At first we had a sort of six o'clock shadow effect, but by the final curtain we had entered properly into the spirit of hairiness. Rosie had big furry hands and sideburns and I had one huge eyebrow right across my forehead. And no one noticed!!! Too busy admiring themselves to notice that two teenage werewolves were handing them their props. Very very funny.

Rosie and I were nearly dead from laughing by the time the curtain came down. The cast went out front to talk to their parents, still in their ridiculous outfits, even Nana. In fact, if I was P. Green's mum I would be worried about ever getting her out of her dog costume.

While they did that we sneaked off home. I have rarely seen anything as funny as Rosie in her school uniform and beret with HUGE sidies and furry hands.

Luckily I managed to skedaddle home without seeing anyone I knew.

Bed

It took me about a year to get my eyebrow off. In the end I had to use nail varnish remover. I've practically removed my forehead.

I must get plenty of beauty sleep and regrow my forehead because I am seeing my boyfriend this weekend. It's only one hundred and eighty hours until he leaves for the Isle of Man with his family for Christmas. And fifty-six of those will be spent sleeping. Unless Libby visits my bed.

Saturday December 18th
Churchill Square
Out with the Ace Gang shopping for Chrimbo presents and lurking around hoping to bump into lads. We were just having a rest on a wall when the Bummers came sauntering past. Jackie Bummer was dressed completely in leather. Leather skirt, jacket, boots, coat... all of it nicked, I bet. She is like a walking crime wave. As a decent citizen I should turn her over to the Old Bill; however, I have my principles and I will never be a snitcher. Especially as snitchers can end up on the wrong end of a duffing incident.

Jackie looked at us like we were snot on legs and said, "Have to dash, little girls, only six shoplifting days to Christmas."

God, they are soooo common and tarty.

4:00 p.m.
At home with my thoughtful Chrimboli gift. I hope Dad

appreciates the ENORMOUS lengths I went to to get him some new socks. I had to wander around very old people's shops for ages to find anything suitable.

5:00 p.m.

I wonder why I haven't heard from SG yet? I've got eight outfits on standby duty and have applied undercoat foundation but it's very tense-making not knowing what is going on.

Living room

Mutti and Vati wrestling about tickling each other. Vati had a very alarming pair of jogging trousers on. I suppose it's nice that they are so affectionate, but I don't like to think of certain people snogging. The Queen, for instance. Imagine the Queen getting to Number Seven with Prince Philip... erlack. Or Herr Kamyer with Hawkeye... erlack, erlack!!! Or Mr and Mrs Next Door in the nuddy-pants.

I must stop this and think of something normal. I might have to go and rub myself with salt to get myself clean again.

Mutti said, "Oh, by the way, when you were in town that really good-looking boy came round. What's his name?"

My face had gone all rigid.

Mutti went on, "You know, the older Jennings boy... he's in that band you go to see... is it the Bob Wilsons or something?"

The Bob Wilsons!!! OhymyGod, ohmyGod. I must go to my room immediately.

As I left the room Mutti said, "I thought he was really tasty. He said would you ring him."

Then Vati got hold of her and he was sort of tickling her with his beard and growling like a lion in jogging trousers.

Bedroom

The Sex God has seen my dad's beard and trousers. He has been exposed to my family. He might even have spoken to Libby. She may have mentioned poo. Will he ever forgive me?

Phoned the Sex God.

"Hi."

"Er, Robbie, I'm really, really, really sorry about my parents, they're just... you know... I'm really sorry."

He laughed. "Your dad is quite cool."

"Pardon?"

Sunday December 19th

Went to band rehearsal again. I have perfected the art of head-nodding and doing my nails at the same time. Dom was looking at me a bit funny, especially as he caught me nodding along to the music when they weren't actually playing any. But at least he has been able to mend his drum. You can still see a slight foot shape in it, though, which in my opinion adds a hint of *je ne sais quoi* to an otherwise ordinary drum kit. At the end the other lads' girlfriends turned up. Mia said hi to me and then, "We're going to the Phoenix bar, are you coming?"

Robbie said, "Well, I'm a bit shattered so we won't." But I knew he really meant that I was officially too young to go.

Pooo!!!

It's a shame that my internal maturiosity is not recognised by the constabulary.

Monday December 20th

I haven't had much time to see the Ace Gang as I have been hanging out with Robbie. How cool is that? Double cool with knobs, that is how cool. Sometimes we talk in between snogging. Well, mostly he talks because I think it is safer that way, and besides I have lots of other things to worry about while he is chatting on about The Stiff Dylans and world peace and so on. Things like avoiding nostril flair, or nip nip eruption, or even as happened the other night, uncontrollable desires to start "Let's go down the disco" dancing when he put some classical music on.

Rang Jas to catch up. "Hey. What has the Ace Gang been up to?"

"We only saw you yesterday, Georgia."

9:35 p.m.
But I know the Ace Gang had a group outing to the cinema last night because Ellen came round to show me her Instamatic photos. How keen is that? To take photos at the cinema. They got thrown out and I'm not surprised. No one would have been able to see the screen with Sven and Dave the Laugh wearing their Christmas antlers.

The gang have probably missed me A LOT, even though they haven't said so.

Ellen said it was "fun" and "a laugh". I didn't ask her about Dave the Laugh, but she told me anyway, about a zillion times... that they are "an item". Huh. Who cares?

Midnight

I noticed in the photos that in addition to his antlers, Dave the L. was wearing the comedy red nose that he wore when he told me he loved me and I accidentally fell over and kissed him. But accidental snogging and red bottomosity are yesterday's news.

Furry Baby Jesuses

Wednesday December 22nd
11:00 a.m.

The Sex God has gone off to the Isle of Man with Tom and the rest of his family. Then he goes straight off on tour of Och-aye land and Prestan-a-gogogogogo land (Wales).

We spent our last night together at his house because his parents were away. It was really groovy with *mucho* ear nibbling and snogging *extraordinaire*. I'm getting the hang of hands now (mine, I mean). I don't just let them dangle about, I give them lots to do. Hair stroking and back stroking and so on. (His hair and his back, not mine.) I think that snogging keeps me in tip-top physical condition. I may suggest to Ms Stamp that she put it into the training schedule for games. Hang on a minute, though... she might want to join in...

When the Sex God and I had to part (which took about an hour and a half because I kept coming out of my door after he had said goodbye and we would do all the goodbye stuff again), he handed me a small package and said, "Don't do anything too loonie while I am away, gorgeous. Here is something for you for Christmas. I'll get you something else from Scotland or Wales." Which is nice.

Unless he gets me a sporran. Or a tartan bikini. Shut up, shut up, brain. It's only because I am full of sadnosity, probably.

I told Jas and she said, "Tom gave me a locket that has a photo of me and him in it that we took at a booth in Seaworld. It's got a backdrop of sea creatures and so on."

I said, "I hope you didn't make any dolphins be in it, because they have hard enough lives as it is, without being made to get into photo booths with you and Tom."

I was quite tearful after SG left. I hope he will like the identity bracelet I got him with my name on. Jas said I should have had *his* name engraved on it, which is what she did with Tom's.

Phoned Jas again. "Jas, why have you put Tom's name on his identity bracelet? Doesn't he already know who he is?"

She sighed like someone who is incredibly full of wisdomosity, which is ironic, and said, "What if he was unconscious or something and no one knew who he was?"

"And you think 'Tom' would do the trick, then?"

She said, "I have to go now." But I don't think she really did have to go.

I will put the little package that SG gave me for a Chrimboli gift under my bed.

12:30 p.m.

Poo. I suppose I will have to get used to being a pop widow. I have to develop my own interests. I must use the time he is away usefully and wisely. I hope it snows early next term and then I can try out the hilariosity of my new idea *vis-à-vis* glove animal and snow blindness.

1:00 p.m.

I wonder how much money I will need to go to America? I've got some money saved up, if I can find my bank book.

1:20 p.m.
Hmm. £15.50.

1:30 p.m.

If I am saving up for Hamburger-a-gogo I can't use money to buy any more Chrimboli prezzies. I will have to be creative.

Luckily I'm very artistic, as everyone knows. Miss Berry, the art teacher, thinks I have a special talent. Not for art, though, sadly. She said I had a special talent for wasting everyone's time. Which is a bit harsh.

I am going to start making my Christmas gifts out of colourful materials and a needle and cotton.

10:00 p.m.

I made some carrot twins for Libby. Two nicely carved carrots with rather attractive gingham headscarves and cloaks on. And for Mutti, a pair of sleep glasses. I cut the spectacle shape out of some fun fur fabric and attached an elastic band. I think she will love and appreciate them, but you can never tell.

As a thoughtful and forgiving gift at this special time of year, I took Naomi's pregnancy smock that I had spent many, many minutes making over to Mr and Mrs Across the Road's house. It has got tiny bows on it and four leg holes, which is unusual in a pregnancy smock. I left it on the doorstep with a note saying, "Best wishes from one who only wishes there to be love and peace in the world."

Saturday December 25th
Christmas Day

Woke up to quite a few prezzies. Libbs climbed in my bed and we opened things together. I am very nearly quite fond of my Mutti and Vati. Vati gave me some CDs I actually wanted!!! Libby LOBED her carrot twins and dumped Mr Potato into the dustbin of life. (Which is just as well, as he was all crinkled and green.)

Mum, in a rare moment of sanity, has bought me a really good bra... which fits and is actually quite nice. Not too thrusting and not too shopping-baggy. Even when I jump up and down, there is very little ad hoc jiggling. Perhaps now I will be able to dance free and wild, with no danger of knocking anyone out with my nunga-nungas.

No sign of snow yet, although it is very very nippy noodles.

1:00 p.m.

M and D and Libbs have gone to visit miscellaneous loons, so I have a private moment to open SG's gift.

It's a compilation tape of songs that he has recorded solo, and it's got "For Georgia, with love, Robbie" written on the little cover thing. In years to come I will be on TV saying, "Yes, Robbie did write the track 'Oh Gorgeous One' for me. Likewise 'Cor, What a Smasher' and 'Phwoar'."

1:30 p.m.

Hmm. There isn't a track called "Oh Gorgeous One" or "Cor, What a Smasher". There are tracks about endangered species and one about Vincent Van Gogh. Not exactly dance extravaganza music, more, it has to be said, music for slitting your wrists to.

2:00 p.m.

I love him for his seriosity.

3:30 p.m.

Big, big news breaking. And no, it is not that Father Christmas is just Dad in a crap white beard (even though that bit is true too). After Christmas lunch, Mr Across the Road dashed over and had a brandy with Dad because... Naomi is in labour!

I said, "Quickly, we must get her on a donkey and head for Bethlehem!" But they all looked at me in that looking-at way that adults have when they do not comprehend the enormity of my hilariosity.

I phoned Jas to let her know the joyful good news. "Naomi is having some furry Baby Jesuses."

"*Non.*"

"*Mais oui.*"

"What shall we do?"

I said, "You get the donkey and I'll sort out the snacks."

4:00 p.m.

Angus is in (even for him) a very bad mood. He's been doing slam dancing in the kitchen to Christmas carols playing on the radio (i.e. he just throws himself against things for no reason). When "Away in a Manger" came on he leaped out of the sink and up on to the plate rack, and then just sort of tap-danced his way along. Four plates and a soup tureen bit the dust.

4:30 p.m.

Decided to take Angus out for a Christmas walk to help him work off his frustration and also ensure that we have something to eat our dinner from. I'm under orders to keep him on his lead in case his inner cat pain drives him to beat up little dogs.

4:35 p.m.

As I was leaving Libby said, "I want to come."

Auntie Kath in Blackpool sent her an all-in-one leopard costume jumpsuit. It's got a tail and ears and whiskers and so on. Libby has had it on all day. Cute.

5:00 p.m.

We had to turn back and get Angus's spare lead because Libby is a cat as well. I hope I don't bump into anyone I know.

5:30 p.m.

It takes over half an hour to get out of the garden. Libby goes so slowly on her hands and knees.

Once I got her to move on, Angus found something

disgusting to dig up. What sort of people bury manky old bits of clothing in other people's gardens?

5:45 p.m.
So that is where Dad's fishing socks went. I remember Dad saying to Mum, "Have you seen my fishing socks?" and Mum saying, "They've probably gone out for a bit of a walk." Because they were so pingy pongees. Even Angus has reburied them.

6:00 p.m.
Angus managed to shake me off the end of his lead by heading straight for a lamp post at eighty miles an hour and swerving at the last minute. Now he is prancing around on Mr Next Door's wall. Now and again he lies down and dangles a paw near them.

Snowy and Whitey have gone completely loopy now. Whitey leaped up and missed Angus's paw and crashed into the wall, but Snowy kept leaping and leaping and Angus was raising his paw slightly higher and higher.

In the end, Angus biffed Snowy mid-leap, right over on to his back. You'd think that Angus would be a bit miserable, or quiet even, as his beloved sex kitten gives birth to another man's kittens. But no, he is an example to us all. I don't know what of.

6:05 p.m.
Sheer stupidity leaps to mind.

In my bedroom
7:00 p.m.
Uh-oh, Mr Across the Road came and banged on our door. I looked down the stairs as Vati answered. It was weird, actually, because usually Mr Across the Road can rave on for England but he didn't seem to be able to speak. He just gestured with his hand for us to follow him. Perhaps he has taken up mime as a Christmas hobby.

We all trailed over to his house. I don't know why I am supposed to be interested. In fact, I thought as a mark of solidarity with Angus I would refuse to go. But I quite wanted to see the kittens.

Angus was on the wall and tapped my head with a paw as I went by. I said, "I'm sorry about this, Angus."

He just yawned and lay on his back chewing his lead.

7:10 P.M.

When we got into his kitchen, Mr Next Door took us to Naomi. He didn't say a word. And Mrs Next Door was just staring down at the cat basket like there was something horrible in it.

Naomi was lying in the basket like the Queen of Sheba, surrounded by kittens. Seven of them...

All of them look like miniature Anguses!!!! Honestly! They all have his markings and everything. This is quite literally a bloody miracle!

10:00 P.M.

A long, long night of Mr and Mrs Across the Road coming across and saying, "Why? Oh why??" and "How?" and occasionally, *"Why?* And *how?"*

In the end they worked out that Angus must have sneaked into Naomi's love parlour before his trouser-snake addendums were, you know... adjusted. Super-Cat!!! He is without doubt the 007 of the cat world.

Sunday December 26th
Boxing Day

The tiny(ish) kittykats are so gorgey. Jas came over and Libby and Jas and I went to visit. Mr and Mrs Across the Road let us in, but were very grumpy about it and were tutting and carrying on. Mr Next Door kept calling Angus "that thing". Which was a bit uncalled for.

And Mrs Next Door said, "Two hundred guineas, she cost us, and for this to happen with a... with a..."

"Proud, heroic Scottish wildcat?" I asked.

"No, with an out of control... *beast*!"

They're just a bit overcome with joy at the moment, but I am sure they will come round in a few thousand years.

Even though they are only a few hours old Angus and Naomi's kittycats are not what you would call the usual sort of kittykat. They haven't even opened their eyes yet, but they are already biting each other and spitting.

I used my womanly charms (which Jas rather meanly said made me look like an axe murderer), and begged Mr and Mrs Next Door to let Angus at least lick his offspring.

3:00 p.m.

Eventually they said he could if he was kept on his lead at all times.

He strutted around purring like a tank (two tanks) biffing the kittykats with his head and licking Naomi. Awww.

That is what I want me and the Sex God to be like. Not necessarily including the bottom-exposing thing that Angus and Naomi go in for A LOT.

Tuesday December 28th

Robbie has phoned me eight times!!!

It's a bit weird because there is always someone around earwigging. Dad's got ears like a bat. (I'll surprise him one day by walking into the front room while he is hanging upside down from the light fitting.) When I was talking to Rosie about how to put your tongue behind your back teeth when you smile because it makes you look sexier he came bursting out of the kitchen and said, "Are you going to be talking rubbish on the phone for much longer, because I want to make a call myself this century."

I said, patiently, "Vati, as I have pointed out many, many times, if you would have the decency to buy me my own mobile phone in keeping with the rest of the universe, then I wouldn't have to use this prehistoric one in the hall." But he just ignored me as usual.

Wednesday December 29th

I arranged with Robbie that he would call me at four o'clock today (as opposed to Isle of Man time, which is about 1948, according to Robbie. I think they still have steam trains). This is the cunning plan we made, in order to be able to say what we like to each other (for example, "You are the most Sex-Goddy thing on legs, I want to suck your shirt, etc., etc."). I told Robbie the telephone number of the phone box down the road and he is going to ring me there.

In the phone box
4:00 p.m.
Mark Big Gob went by with his midget girlfriend. Rosie didn't believe me when I told her how very very tiny Mark's girlfriend is, but she is. You could quite easily strap a bowl of peanuts to her tiny head and use her as a sort of snacks table at parties. That is how small she is.

Mark Big Gob gave me a hideous wink as he went by. It's

hard to believe that he actually dumped me before I was going to dump him for being so thick. How annoying is that? Vair vair annoying, but... then the phone rang and my beloved Sex God of the universe and beyond spoke to me.

At Jas's
5:00 p.m.

Jas's mutti and vati are out and we are practising for our trip to Froggyland by eating a typico French peasant meal: *pomme de terre* and *les* baked beans *avec le* sauce *de* tomato. Oh, and of course, *de rigueur*... we wore our berets and stripy T-shirts.

I said, "I 'ope that Gorgey Henri can control his passion for me when we reach Paree."

Jas was also wearing what she imagines are sexy shades. She's wrong, though – they don't make her look French, they make her look blind.

She said, "Gorgey Henri does not have *la* passion for you, he thinks you are *la* stupid schoolgirl."

"Oh, *mais non, ma* idiot, *au contraire* he thinks I am *le* genius."

We both had a lot of frustrated snogging energy so we

had to do "Let's go down the disco" dancing on Jas's bed for about an hour. We were pretending we were in a French disco inferno, which means we yelled, *"Mon Dieu!"* *"Zut alors!!!"* and *"Merde!"* A LOT.

Midnight
I think I may actually have broken my neck from doing too much head banging.

Thursday December 30th
Woke up this morning and there was a sort of weird light in the bedroom. When I opened the curtains I discovered that it had snowed overnight!!!

Mr Next Door was already up wearing ludicrous snow wear – bobble hat, duffle coat and rubber trousers, clearing his path with a shovel. He got to the end of the path near the gate and then had a breather to survey his handiwork. He probably imagines he is like Nanuk of the North.

It's a shame if he does, because as he walked back up his newly cleared path, he went flying on a slippy bit and ended up skidding along on his rubber trousers.

Happy days!!

11:45 a.m.

Oh *trés sportif*. We are going to have the Winter Olympics! All the gang are going to meet up on the back fields for snow fun and frolics.

"What are you going to wear?" I asked Rosie.

"Short, black leather skirt, new knee-boots and a LOT of lip gloss."

"That is not exactly sensible winter wear."

"I know," she said. "I may freeze to death, but I will look fabbity fab fab."

She is not wrong. I may have to rifle through my wardrobe for glamorous *après-ski* wear.

I don't know why I am bothering, really, as the Sex God is not here, but you have to keep up appearances for good humourosity and fashionosability's sake.

Phoned Jas. "Jas, what are you wearing for the sledging and snow sports extravaganza?"

"Well, I was thinking snug and warm."

"Well, you can't just wear your huge winter knickers, Jas."

"Hahahaha-di-haha. What are you wearing?"

"Hmmm... ski pants, ankle boots and I think roll-neck

top and leather jacket. Oh, and waterproof eye make-up in case of a sudden snowstorm."

12:00 p.m.
I think snow wear quite suits me. My hat de-emphasises on the conk front which is always a good thing. Lashings and lashings of mascara and lip gloss for extra warmth and I am just about ready.

I managed to sneak out of the house without Libby hearing me. I love her, but she is being a pain about this cat costume thing – she won't take it off and it is beginning to be a bit on the pingy pongo side.

1:00 p.m.
I was a bit late because Angus kept following me and I had to chuck snowballs at him to dodge him.

Dave the Laugh, Ellen, Jools, Rollo, Mabs, Sam, Rosie, Sven, Jas and some lads I didn't know were sledging down a hill on the back fields. Well, apart from Ellen, who was in a ditherama at the top of the hill. She was not exactly dressed for downhill sledging (her skirt was about half an inch short and she was wearing false eyelashes). But neither was anybody else exactly dressed for downhill sledging, and that wasn't stopping *them*. As the rest of them whizzed down the hill in a sledge sandwich – boy-girl-boy-girl sledge – Ellen was fiddling with her hair and gazing down the hillside.

She said, "I've been going out with him for nearly three weeks now. In hours, that is... er... a lot."

I didn't say anything.

"Do you think he likes me as much as I like him?"

I didn't say anything. I am keeping my wisdomosity to myself.

"Do you think I should ask him?"

"What?"

"Ask him how much he likes me?"

"Er... I don't know... I mean, boys are, you know, not girls with trousers on, are they?" I astonished even myself with my outburst of extreme wisdomosity. Ellen looked at me all blinky and expectant, like I was a fortune-teller or something. I felt a bit like that bloke in *Julius Caesar*, the one who says, "Beware the idle of March."

Ellen asked me why she shouldn't ask him. Good question. Good. "Er... because Dave might feel like you are putting pressure on his individualosity."

"His individualosity?"

"Yes."

"What, by asking him if he likes me as much as I like him?"

"That's the one."

"Well, what should I do instead, then?"

"Be cool, and, you know... er, funny and relaxed... and fun and happening and... er... so on." What am I talking about? Alarmingly, Ellen seemed to think I made sense.

By this time, Dave and the gang had struggled back up the hill with the sledge. Dave said, "Nippy noodles, isn't it?" He was smiling at me. He's got a really cool, sort of naughty, smile. It makes you think of lip nibbling. "Look, girls, I couldn't put my hands down the front of your jumpers, could I? To warm them up? There would be nothing rudey-dudey in it, you understand. To me your nunga-nungas are just a pair of giant mittens."

Ellen looked a bit puzzled. As I have said many times, I wonder if Ellen is quite a good enough laugh for Dave the Laugh.

Friday December 31st
New Year's Eve
2:00 p.m.

The Ace Gang are going to SEVEN parties, but as a mark of respect Jas and I have decided not to go with them. We are having our own widows' celebration.

Actually, I would rather go out than be cooped up with Jas, but I know that Dave the Laugh will be there and I don't want to entice my bottom into another display of redness. Especially as I have got snogging withdrawal VERY badly.

11:00 p.m.

This is the glorious start to my New Year...

Jas and I stayed in and watched people on television kissing each other and waving their kilts around. Jas is staying over and my so-called parents and Libby have gone out to some sad party. They actually asked if I would like to go with them. When I indicated that I would rather set fire to myself they left me alone. However, as a special treat Mum got us some food. I said to Dad, "Jas is more of a champagne girl, really, so if you could just get a few bottles. I think that would make our fabulous evening go with a swing."

He didn't even bother to reply.

On the stroke of midnight, Jas said, "Shall we?"

And I said, "Jas, don't even think about asking me to snog you."

She got all huffy. "No, I wasn't going to. I was going to say, shall we have a celebratory disco inferno dancing experience with the aid of soft toys

12:30 a.m.

And a happy New Year to one and all!!!

Our New Year "Let's go down the disco" experience, with the aid of Charlie Horse and Teddy as partners, was actually quite good fun on the funosity scale. Although I was slightly worried about Jas because she did actually snog Teddy.

She said, "I'm pretending it's Tom."

I said, "Teddy is very very like Tom in many ways – his furry ears, for instance."

We were just biffing each other with Charlie and Teddy when the phone rang.

It was SG and Tom phoning from the Isle of Man. Yeahhhhhhh!!!

The Sex God said, "Happy New Year, gorgeous, see you

soon." Then he had to go and toss dwarfs or whatever it is they do in the Isle of Man to celebrate. I read that they still have birching there, so anything could happen.

Jas was Mrs Moony Knickers after talking to Hunky, and we just went to watch people snogging and singing on TV.

1:15 a.m.
Ho hum pig's bum.

When my "family" got home, as a hilarious treat, Dad had brought home a bit of coal. He said, "It's called 'first footing'." It should be called "first loon in". He burst in like the original red-faced loon and said, "Happy New Year." Then he tried to hug me and Jas. We beat him off with Teddy and Charlie Horse and then Libby joined in and hung on to his beard, as Jas and I made a bid for freedom to my room.

Sunday January 2nd
11:30 a.m.
To keep our spirits up, Jas and I made a list of things to take to Froggyland with us.

"We are going to have to hire an extra ferry to take our hair products over," I told her.

Monday January 3rd

2:00 p.m.

Moped around at Jas's. We are united in widow sadness. We listened to sad songs and practised being interviewed on Michael Parkinson. Jas is hopeless at it. When I (as Parky) asked her what her hopes for the future were, she said, "World peace and more freely available organic vegetables." How interesting is that?

Not, is the correct answer.

Ooooh, I am soooo bored and lonely. NOTHING happens around here.

I lolloped home up our street. At least Angus is happy, though. He is lolling around on the wall overlooking Mr and Mrs Across the Road. He is a very proud dad. I wonder how long it will be before we are allowed to name the kittykats? Mr and Mrs Across the Road are being very unreasonable about it all, and won't discuss it.

When I got back to the house Mum said, "Robbie rang you. The number's beside the phone."

I got the usual jelloid knickers (and added leg tremblers and a quick spasm of quivering-a-gogo).

Should I phone him back or just wait for him to phone again? I must think.

Perhaps if I ate some chocolate orange egg it would calm me down. There was one left under the tree.

The front room was a nightmare of beardosity. Vati had some of his mates from work and Uncle Eddie round watching the football. He was slurping beer and being all jolly. "Georgia, this is Mike, Nick, Paul and Bingo... the lads!"

Lads? Since when were lads 85? And a half.

The great tragedy is that the "lads" are going to be forming a football team. I was about to say, "Should men in your physical condition hurl themselves around a football pitch?" But then Dad dropped his bombshell.

"Georgia, what is this with Robbie? Why is he phoning you all the time and coming round? How old is he?"

I said with great dignosity, "Father, I am afraid I can't discuss my private life with you as I have a date with *Lord of the Flies.*"

He said, "Who's he, then?" And the "lads" all laughed.

I said, "It is a book by William Golding that I have to study for my homework."

I got out of the room fast. As I went up the stairs I could hear the "lads" raving on. "They don't know they're born these days, do they? Reading books... French... In my day any kid in the street with two ears was a sissy..."

I heard Dad say, "Our school still had capital punishment." And they all laughed like bearded loons. Which they are.

10:30 p.m.
I can't phone Robbie because then Dad will know that I am phoning him and that will make him even more full of suspiciosity.

11:00 p.m.
Lord of the Flies is so boring... and so weird. I always thought boys were very very strange, but I didn't think they would start eating each other. Bloody hell, I must make sure I never end up on an island with a bunch of boys!

Wednesday January 5th

Tom arrived back from the family Chrimboli. Jas was ridiculously excited. She is a fairweather pal, because I know

I will be dumped now that her so-called boyfriend is back. And SG isn't back until next Tuesday.

Friday January 7th

Snowed like billy-o overnight. Angus leaped out of the front door like he normally does and completely disappeared from view, the snow was so deep. He loves it and is leaping and sneezing about in the back garden.

Rosie and the gang are going sledging down the back fields. But I am not in the mood for winter sports until my beloved returns. I explained this to Rosie and she said, "Make love, not war." What is she talking about?

Besides, I saw Ellen and Dave the Laugh holding hands down at Churchill Square yesterday and it made me feel a bit funny. I don't know why.

Saturday January 8th

10:00 a.m.

Robbie phoned from East Jesus (or Prestan-a-gogogogoch... anyway, somewhere in Welsh country). The gigs are going really well, but he is shattered and can't talk much because his throat is sore from singing. He said, "I miss you, gorgeous."

Boo hoo, this is so sad.

Still, he is back on Tuesday. I may distract myself by doing snogging exercises to limber up.

Sunday January 9th

My exercise regime: doing my yoga sun salute ten times and then pucker-ups (like Mick Jagger) forty times.

6:00 p.m.

Stalag 14 starts again tomorrow. Shall we never be free? On the bright side, the snow gives a very good comedy opportunity for an outing of glove animal.

8:00 p.m.

Rang around the Ace Gang.

"Rosie."

"*D'accord.* It's me."

"Is it you?"

"Yes."

"Goodbye."

"Goodbye."

Rang back. "I'll just say this: Operation Glove Animal and

Snow Blindness."

"Pip, pip."

Phoned Jools and Mabs and Ellen, who are all prepared. Then I phoned Mrs Useless Knickers. "Jas, it's snowing. Prepare glove animal."

"Oh no, we'll only get bad conduct marks immediately."

"Yes, but think of the hilariosity of it, Jas."

"But..."

"Jas, if you can't think of the hilariosity, think of the severe duffing you will get if you don't do it."

Monday January 10th

Rendez-voused at the bottom of the hill, where we all clipped on our glove ears under our berets and put on sunglasses. As we bobbled up the hill, Rosie was nearly going to the piddly-diddly department on the spot as she was laughing so much.

8:55 a.m.

Mabs did actually walk into a tree because she couldn't see through her sunglasses. Oh, how we laughed.

As we approached the school gate, we could see Hawkeye

lurking. We tucked our ears up under our berets, but kept our sunglasses on.

Hawkeye tutted and ferreted at us as we walked by. She said, "What is this nonsense?"

I said, "It's to prevent snow blindness, Mrs Heaton."

She said, "It's a pity there's no way to prevent stupidity." Which I think is quite bad manners for someone who is teaching the youth of today, but I didn't say so.

Tuesday January 11th
8:25 a.m.
Sex God back today AND the kittykats have opened their eyes!!! They are soooooo sweet and, as I explained to Jas, "Now they can see to fight properly."

9:00 p.m.
Robbie came round to see me as soon as he got back. How cool is that?

When he arrived at the door, Dad called me and then he and Mum spent about a million years raising their eyebrows and looking "wise". And trying to be modern and to get on with the youth, which is ludicrous.

Vati started to talk about Kiwi-a-gogo land. I said, "Fancy going for a walk, Robbie? I'm a bit... er... hot."

And Dad said, "It's pitch black and about minus seven outside." He was going to go on and on, but then I saw Mutti give him a "look", a "modern, understanding mum look", that said, "Come on, Bob, remember when you were that age?" Which is a physical impossibility for my dad. How very very embarrassing. Shut up, stop looking, shut up, shut up.

Vati said, "Be back by eleven."

Oh, how sad and embarrassing.

Robbie took my hand and once we got away from our house into the dark street he snogged me. Yipppppeeeee!

Midnight

Cor, bloody nippy noodles out there. But I have my love to keep me warm (that and the extra pair of knickers I put on).

I must say, I think my puckering exercises have paid off, because I haven't got any aches or pains. Robbie told me about being on tour. He said he wasn't sure that he really liked it. But I'm sure that is just a phase he is going through. Once we are squillionaires he will change his mind.

1:00 a.m.

I wonder why he asked me if I liked the countryside? Maybe he wants us to go and snog in the great outdoors?

Wednesday January 12th

8:15 a.m.

Dad brought me a cup of tea in bed this morning! I said, "Vati, why are you waking me up in the middle of the night? Are you on fire?"

I had to pull the sheets up really quickly in case he could see any bits of my body. He hung around after he had put the cup down. He was sort of all red and beardy.

"Georgia, I'm not trying to... well, I know you have your own mind... and Robbie seems like a really, you know, great bloke... but he's, you know, a big lad and well... well, it's just that... well, don't get too serious too soon."

What in the name of Buddha's bra is he going on about now?

Then he ruffled my hair (very, very annoying) and went out. Robbie's a "big lad". What does that mean?

I really will have to break the news soon that I am going off on tour to Hamburger-a-gogo land with The Stiff Dylans.

Vati obviously doesn't think I am capable of maturiosity. But he is wrong.

Wrongy wrong wrong.

I wonder how much money I will need for *le* gay Paree weekend, for essentials and so on? I might test the water *vis-à-vis* spondulicks for my trip to Hamburger-a-gogo land with a simple enquiry about available finance for Froggyland.

Front room
7:30 p.m.
Vati was actually doing a press-up when I came in. I hope he is insured.

"Vati."

"Urgh."

"Can I have £220 for my weekend in Paris, please?"

I thought I was going to have to use my first aid skills on Vati. Which would have been a shame as I only know how to force a boiled sweet out of someone if they are choking to death.

Saturday January 15th

The snow has melted, thank the Lord. It is so hard on the elderly. However, they can be quite suspicious, the elderly. I offered to go shopping for Mr and Mrs Next Door yesterday in case they were frightened of going out. And they were quite surly about it. I said to Mr Next Door, "I couldn't help noticing that you are even more unsteady than usual on your feet in this kind of weather." And he told me to go annoy someone else, which is a bit rude, I think.

2:00 p.m.

As everyone is out, SG came round. We snogged for thirty-five minutes without stopping (I timed it because I could see the clock over Robbie's shoulder). Rosie rang while he was here and said they were having an indoor(!) barbecue at her house tonight. The theme is "sausages". Robbie couldn't make it, though, because he is busy.

Bye bye, dreamboat.

8:30 p.m.

I didn't go to the sausage extravaganza. Heaven only knows what sausages would bring out in me; I was bad enough at the fish party. I will concentrate on my French vocabulary instead so that I can ask for things in Paris.

9:00 p.m.
Sausage is *saucisson* in French. Shut up, brain.

I am a bit worried because Robbie turned up this afternoon not in his groovy mini, but on a secondhand bike.

11:30 p.m.
I hope he doesn't suggest we go for bike rides together. It is minus a hundred and eighty degrees, and the last time I rode a bike my skirt got caught in the back wheel and I had to walk home in my knickers.

Frogland extravaganza

Monday January 17th
Stalag 14
Quatre days to our Frogland extravaganza
French

M'sieur "call me Henri" really is sooo cool and gorgey. He told us what we are going to do on our school trip to *la belle France* and what we should bring. We're going to stay in Hôtel Gare du Nord and visit the Champs Elysées and the Pompidou Centre. Loads of *très bon* stuff. Madame Slack came in and took all our forms that we had to take home for signing – the forms saying that even if we were set fire to by raving French people, the staff are not responsible, etc. She also said, "Girls, on Saturday there will be a choice of excursion in the morning. You can go on a grand tour of the sewage system of Paris with me, go up the Eiffel Tower with

M'sieur Hilbert or to the Louvre with Herr Kamyer. Please come and sign up for your choice."

As we queued up we argued about which trip to go on as a gang. Jas was the only one who wanted to go down into the sewers. I said to Jas, "What is the point of going down the sewers?"

"Because it is historical and we might learn a lot of stuff we don't know."

I said, "*Au contraire*, we will learn a lot of things we DO know. We will learn that French sewers are like English sewers, only French."

Jas looked like a goggle-eyed ferret.

I explained. "It is just tunnels full of French poo – how different can French poo be from English poo?"

So we are all going up the Eiffel Tower with Gorgey Henri.

Ellen said, "I'm looking forward to going and everything, but I will really miss Dave the Laugh... he's such a..."

I said, "Laugh?"

"Yes," she said, and went all red. Good Lord.

I am, of course, used to being away from the Sex God. He's only been back a week and I'm off to Frogland.

I sometimes wish he was more of a laugh, though. There is a slight danger that underneath his Sex God exterior there lurks a sensible person. He has just bought a bike to save the environment. And it might not stop there... he might possibly buy some waterproofs.

Thursday January 20th

Slim gave us her world famous (not) "Representatives of Great Britain abroad" speech. Apparently we have the weight of the reputation of the British Isles on our shoulders.

I said to Jools: "I'm already tired, and we haven't even got on the coach yet."

Midnight

I've managed to whittle down my necessities to one haversack full. Jas and I are doing sharesies on some things to save space. For instance, I am supplying our hair gel for the weekend and she is supplying moisturiser. I will not be sharing knickers with her, though.

I said *au revoir* to *mon amour*. He came round on his bike

AGAIN, and also (this is the worst bit), he talked to my dad about Kiwi-a-gogo land... and he didn't shoot himself with boredom. In fact, he even asked questions, which proved he had been listening to Vati raving on about Maoris. *Très* weird.

Friday January 21st
Aboard L'esprit
Midday

On our way to *la belle France* at last. If we ever get there it will be *le miracle*, because: a) it is a French ferry and b) we have a madman at the helm. When we set off from Newhaven we went in and out of the quay three times, because the captain forgot to cast off.

1:00 p.m.

Zut alors, we are being tossed about like *les* corks. I may complain to the captain (if he has not been airlifted home to a secure unit) and suggest he stops driving us into eighty-foot waves. Herr Kamyer, dithering champion for the German nation and part-time fool, has just lost his footing and fallen into the ladies' loos.

1:15 p.m.

In the restaurant there is a notice that says, *"Soupe du jour"*, so Rosie said to the French waiter, "Can I have *le soupe du yesterday*, please?" But no one got it.

1:30 p.m.

Staggering around on the decks in gale-force winds.

I could see Captain Mad up in his wheelhouse thing.

1:32 p.m.

The only way to stay upright is to hold the flagpole at the back of the boat.

1:35 p.m.

Why does he keep staring at me? I'm just clinging on to this French flag because I want to live to see Frogland...

Just then the boat lurched violently, and that's when it came off in my hand.

2:30 p.m.

Madame Slack, who until then had been attached to Gorgey Henri for most of the voyage (like a Slack limpet), decided to make a big international thing out of the flag-removing incident.

She gibbered in *le* Frog to Captain Mad, who had come down to the deck (hopefully leaving someone who could drive in his place). They did a lot of pointing and shouting and shrugging.

Incidentally, why has Madame Slack got two huge handbags? She keeps sellotape and a ruler in one and a hankie in the other. Should someone like that be in charge of the youth of today? Is France a nation of handbag fetishists, I wonder? As I said to Jas, "Even Henri has got a little handbag."

Rosie said, "You are definitely going to have to walk the gangplank. *Au revoir, mon amie.*"

"What makes you think Captain Mad could find a gangplank – I'll be amazed if he can find France." But I said it quietly. I didn't want to start the shrugging again.

In the end, Madame Slack called me stupid about a zillion times, which could have upset me, but I know I am really full of geniosity.

I had to apologise to Captain Mad. In French.

4:45 p.m.

Still in this sodding boat, bobbing up and down in the Atlantic or wherever it is we are now.

Suddenly Rosie said, "Land!!! I can see land, thank the Lord!" and got down on her knees. Which was quite funny. It could be Iceland, though, for all we know.

Captain Mad came on the PA system and said, "Ladeez and Jentlemen, ve are now approaching Dieppe."

I said to the gang, "With a bit of luck, he'll manage to dock by tomorrow evening."

9:00 p.m.

Miraculously survived the ferry journey and caught the train to Paris. I think the driver might have been wearing a beret, but we still managed to arrive at Hôtel Gare du Nord, in *le* gay Paree!! Right in the middle of everything.

The lady behind the desk said, "Welcome, I will show you to your rrruuuuuuums." I thought French people were actually being funny when they put on their accent, but they aren't being funny, they are being French. That, as I said to Jas, is why I *aime* them so much.

Gorgey Henri has let the Ace Gang be in the same room

together!!! How fab is he? Usually we get split up in class, but the six of us are back together again. Yes!!! *Les* girls have arrived. It's a really groovy room as well. I have a bed by the window. I lay down on it and said, "Aaahhh, this is the sort of life I will be leading from now on."

Rosie said, "What? Sharing a room with five other women? Are you setting up a lezzie farm?" I had to duff her rather savagely over the head with my pillow.

Jas had brought the photo of Tom and her at Seaworld with her and she put it on the table by the side of her bed. Ellen tried to sneak a book under her pillow, but I saw it.

"What's that?" I asked.

"Oh, it's just a bit of homework I brought with me."

Rosie fished it out and read out the title. "It's called *Black Lace Shoulder*, a story of passion on the high seas." Now we know what sort of homework she is doing: snogging research. It was a semi-naughty book. I flicked through it and found a bit to read to the rest of the gang.

"He captivated women with his fierce, proud face, his lean, well exercised body and his aura of sexuality, wild as that of a stallion."

Rosie said, "That's like Sven."

Jas said, "What, he's like a stallion?"

"Yes."

I said, "A stallion in loons?"

Rosie said, "*Mais oui.*"

"*Quel* number have you got up to now with *le* stallion in loons on the scoring system?" I asked.

"Eight." Upper-body fondling indoors. All of our eyes drifted towards Rosie's basoomas, which, it has to be said, are not gigantic.

Ellen said, "Is it, does it... I mean, are your, erm, nungas... getting bigger?"

Rosie looked down the front of her T-shirt. "I think they are a bit. Not as much as Georgia's, though."

Oh no, here we go. I thought my new nunga-nunga holder had stopped this sort of talk. To change the subject I said to Ellen, "What number have you got up to with Dave?"

She went all red. "Oh, well, you know, he's like really a good, well, kisser."

Yes, as it happens, I do know that he's a really good kisser.

Rosie was all interested now. "Has he touched anything?"

Ellen was about to explode from redness. "Well, he stroked my hair."

We haven't even bothered to put hair-stroking on our snogging scale. If we had, it would have been Minus One.

Out of our bedroom window we can see the streets of Paris and the French-type *garçons*. Some of them look quite groovy, but their trousers are a bit too short. Perhaps this is the French way. I said, "Look, people are wearing berets and they're not even going to school. Unless they still go to school at ninety-four."

Saturday January 22nd
Saturday in Paris
9:30 a.m.

Oh *j'aime* Paris muchly. For brekkie we had hot chocolate and croissant. All the French kids dipped their croissant into their hot chocolate. How cool is that? Yummy scrumboes.

We set off with Gorgey Henri for the Eiffel Tower. I was singing "Fallink in luff again, never vanted to..." until Rosie pointed out that Marlene Dietrich sang that and she was by no means a French person.

Up the Eiffel Tower
11:00 a.m.

Jas and I got split up somehow from the rest of the gang. Well, mainly because Jas was dithering around making me take a photo of her with some French pigeons. How anyone would know they were French pigeons, I don't know. I said to her, "We will have to draw little stripy T-shirts on them when we get the prints back."

Anyway, the others had gone on ahead and we got trapped just in front of a group of French schoolboys of about nine years old. They spent the million years it took climbing the steps looking up our skirts.

Jas was OK because she had her holiday knickers on (same gigantic ones as her daywear in England, but with a frilly bit round the gusset). I, however, had normals on, and so I tried to walk up the stairs with my legs together, which is not easy. Every time I looked behind me I could see the little boys ogling like ogles on ogle tablets.

When we eventually got to the top, Jas said, "It's your fault. You should have worn sensible knickers."

"Jas, *fermez la bouche* or I will *fermer* it for you."

oh la la la gay Paree

2:00 p.m.

We walked along the banks of the Seine in the winter sunshine. There were musicians and so on playing and a bird market. I wanted to take a chaffinch or some lovebirds home with me, but I knew that they'd only last two minutes if Angus got a snack-attack in the middle of the night. As we passed a bloke playing a saxophone underneath one of the arches, he put down the sax and started doing a juggling thing with his hands. It was a bit peculiar, though, because, as I said to Jas, "He hasn't got any balls."

Rosie said, "Oo-er..." which set us off on the uncontrollable laughing fandango.

Jas said, "He must be doing a sort of mime thing." Mime juggling? In the end, unfortunately, we realised that he was actually pretending to juggle my breasts. I am the first to admit that I can be paranoid about my nungas, but in this case it was clear even to Jas that he was a perv. He pointed at my nungas and made a sort of leering, licking smile and then continued his pretend juggling. How disgusting!!

Am I never to be free from the tyranny of my basoomas? I buttoned my coat up as tightly as possible.

La nuit extravaganza

Henri took us down Rue St Denis in the evening and said, "Zis is where the ladeez of the night ply their trade."

Jas said, "I can't see any ladies of the night, all I can see are a load of prostitutes." She astonishes me with her hilarious stupidosity sometimes.

Actually, it should have been called "Rue de Bummer", because all the prozzies looked exactly like the Bummer twins. Only less spotty.

It isn't even just Henri who has a handbag, lots of *les français* men have little handbags. And no one laughs. Weird. I may buy one for Dad, as a souvenir.

Sunday January 23rd

Herr Kamyer has reached the dizzying heights of giddiness since he's been in Paris, even going so far as to wear leisure slacks and a jumper with a koala on it. Jas said kindly, "Perhaps it's a Christmas gift from his mum." But I don't think so. I think he knitted it himself. And I think he is proud of it.

1:00 p.m.

Jas and Rosie keep nipping off to phone Tom and Sven every five minutes.

I would phone Robbie, but I don't really know what to say to him. What if he asks me what I have been doing? What would I say? "I pulled off a French flag, some boys looked up my skirt and finally a bloke with a saxophone juggled my breasts." I wouldn't mean to say any of that, but I know I would blurt it out.

2:15 p.m.

Herr Kamyer has been showing us how to ask for things in shops. I know how to do this already: all you do is ask Gorgey Henri to go and ask for whatever it is you want in the shop. He does, after all, know the language. However, Herr Kamyer thinks we should learn stuff, so he keeps going up to French people and asking for things, which is hilarious in the extreme as a) no one has a clue what he is talking about and b) they wouldn't give him anything anyway, because he is not French.

Oh, I tell a lie. He did manage to get something. He went into the tourist information centre for a map. "I vill be back in a moment, girls, *mit der* map and ve vill proceed to the Champs Elysées."

He came out ten minutes later dithering like a loon with a souvenir walking stick but no map. As I pointed out to Jools, "The tragic thing is that they speak English in the tourist information centre."

Plunging into the Seine photo opportunity

We tried the "Just step back a bit, Herr Kamer, I can't get all your jumper in" tactic on the banks of the Seine. But Herr Kamyer looked back before he moved so he did not plunge into the Seine. And now we really do have a photo of Herr Kamyer in his jumper.

Notre Dame
4:00 p.m.

Very gothic. No sign of hunchbacks, though. So... with a marvellous display of imaginosity (and also after Herr Kamyer, Henri and Madame Slack had gone into the cathedral) the Ace Gang got into their hunchback gear (haversacks under coats). We were getting ready shuffling around and yelling, "The bells, the bells," but then Jas and I stepped on to a bit of green grass verge to take a photo of the Ace Gang being hunchbacks against the romantic backdrop of Notre Dame (*très* historic). Suddenly all hell broke loose. Whistles went and some absolute loon started yelling through a loudspeaker in French at us. Then we were surrounded by blokes in uniforms. I thought we were going to be taken to the Bastille.

I said to Jas, "What have we done? Ask one of them."

She said, "You came top in French, you ask." Unfortunately, I had come top in French only to annoy Madame Slack. I had learned twenty-five words and then made sure I answered every question using only those words.

Just then Henri came running back to save us. He started yelling and shrugging his shoulders and soon everyone was shrugging shoulders. Even the bloke selling birdfood. I don't know what he had to do with it.

I turned to the gang. "Wait for a big group shrug and then run like the wind for sanctuary into Notre Dame. We must beg the priests to save us."

It all got sorted out in the end. The French loon patrol turned out to be park keepers. Sort of like park Elvises.

Apparently you are not allowed to step on their grass, because it drives them insane.

Madame Slack gave her world famous "Once again a few bad apples have spoilt the reputation of England" lecture and gave us all bad conduct medals. I mean marks.

I said to Jas, "You would think that she would encourage us to bring history to life, but oh no, *au contraire*, we are pilloried on the spike of... er... life."

9:30 p.m.

Henri took us out to a restaurant tonight. It was really groovy, apart from some old drunk at the piano who kept moaning on about "*Je ne regrette rien*". Ellen asked, "What is he going on about?"

I said, "He's saying in French that he doesn't regret a thing, which he quite clearly should. He should regret having started this song, for one thing."

Henri said he was a famous French singer. Good Lord.

Very, very funny evening. There was a notice on our table saying what you could have to eat. It said "Frogs' legs" at the top. When the waiter came he spoke English (sort of). "Good evening, Mademoiselle, what can I get you?"

I said, "*S'cuse moi*, have you got frogs' legs?"

He smiled. "Yes, M'selle."

So I said, "Well, hop off and get me a sandwich, then."

We laughed for about a million years. Even the waiter thought it was funny(ish). However, Madame Slack heard what had happened and said we were "giddy".

Monday January 24th
Last morning in gay Paree

Sitting by myself in a café because the Ace Gang have gone off to look at some French boys. I even ordered a cup of coffee for myself. And a croissant. Well, actually, it looks more like an egg sandwich (because it is an egg sandwich), but at least it's not a walking stick.

Pompidou Centre
Midday

You can't move for white-faced loons in the area around the centre. Some of them just stand still for ages and ages, painted all white like a statue. Then when you are really bored from looking at them, they slowly move a finger, or lift a leg, and then go back to being still. And people throw coins in their hats for that. I said to Rosie, "What is the point of mime artists? Why don't they just tell you what they want?"

Then I noticed that a gorgey *garçon* was watching me watching the white-faced loons. I kept catching him looking at me. He was cute. *Trés* cute. And his trousers were relatively normal. And he wasn't wearing a beret. And he was handbag-free.

He caught my eye and smiled quite a dreamy smile. He was very intense-looking, with incredibly dark curly hair. However, I am a red bottom-free zone and I was just about to ignore him when he went off.

Ah well. *C'est la guerre*, as they say here, although what the railway station has to do with anything, I don't know. (Or is that *gare*? Oh, I don't know. As I say to Madame Slack, French is a foreign language to me.)

Five minutes later

The gorgey French boy came back and brought me a red rose!! He said, "For the most beeootiful girl," kissed my hand and then went off into the crowd.

Honestly.

The Ace Gang were dead impressed. We discussed it for ages. It didn't fit into the snogging scale anywhere. And it wasn't a "see you later". Was I supposed to follow him? Should I have done something erotic with the rose?

As I have said with huge wisdomosity many times, boys the world over are a bloody mystery.

Au reviour

We got on the train and said *"Auf Wiedersehen"* to the city of romance. We have our memories to take home with us. More importantly, we also have our HUGE comedy berets.

We found them in a souvenir shop in the station that sold musical Eiffel Towers, nuddy-pants cancan dancers and other sophisticated gifts. The berets are gigantic and they are wired around the rim, so that they stick out about a foot from your head. Excellent!!! They are quite hilarious in the extreme. We each got one. I can't wait to wear them to school. They make the lunchpack berets seem traditional by comparison.

When we got on the train, Madame Slack went off to the teachers' compartment, probably to chat with Gorgey Henri about handbags they had known and loved. We took the opportunity to try on our new berets. All six of us leaned out of our carriage window wearing our gigantic berets as the train pulled out. We were yelling "AU REVOIR, PARIS! WE LOVE YOU ALL!!!"

And guess what? The people on the platform all waved and cheered. They were shouting, *"Bonne chance!"* I think.

I asked Jas, as we tucked into our cheesy snacks for the journey. "Do you think that the French-type people think we really like our berets?"

She said, "No, I think they think we are English people and therefore not normal."

"How could they think that?" asked Rosie.

Then I noticed that Rosie was wearing a false moustache as well as her beret.

Oh, how we laughed.

On the ferry heading home

Uneventful trip home because we had a normal captain (i.e., English).

Also we had chips. A LOT.

I was quite overcome when we saw the white cliffs of Dover, until I realised we aren't going to Dover and they are just some crappy old white cliffs of somewhere else.

Midnight

Arrived home to my loving family. As I came up the drive, Angus shot over the wall and gave me a playful bite on the ankle as he passed. I opened the door and yelled, *"C'est moi! Your daughter is home again, crack open the fatted calf and..."*

Angus had pushed his way in first and Dad started yelling, "Get that bloody cat out! This house is full of fleas."

I said sternly to Angus, "Angus, stay out of the house, it is full of fleas!" But the Loonleader didn't think it was funny. Even though it is.

12:10 a.m.

Libby was pleased to see me, at least. She woke up when I came in and said, "Heggo Gingey."

She made me a card with a drawing of a cat band on the front. Angus is the lead singer, although why he is upside down, I don't know. The audience is little mice and voles in disco wear.

By the time I had unpacked my bag, Libby had fallen back

to sleep in my bed with her "fwends". She is so lovely when she is sleeping and I gave her a kiss on her cheek. I wonder how I will get on without her when I go to America. It made me feel a bit weepy, actually. I must have boat-lag.

Just as I was dropping off into snoozeland, Mutti came in. I think she might have had a couple of glasses of *vino tinto*, because she looked a bit flushed.

"Hello darling, welcome back. How was France?"

"*Fantastique.*"

"This came for you." And she handed me a letter. In the Sex God's handwriting!! Wow and wowzee wow!

Mutti came and sat on my bed.

"So, did you have a fab time?"

"*Oui, Très sportif.* Night, night."

"Did you see the Eiffel Tower? It's amazing at night, isn't it? Was it all lit up?"

Oh, good grief. I know she was being a nice mutti and everything, but I wanted to read my Sex God notelet. I said kindly, "Mum, I'm a bit boat-lagged, I'll tell you all about it in the morning."

She touched Libby's cheek and then she touched mine.

"Don't grow up too fast, love." She looked all tearful.

What is the matter with grown-ups? They are always banging on about how childish you are and telling you to grow up and so on, and then when you do, they start blubbing.

After she'd left I ripped open my letter.

Dear Georgia,

Welcome home, snog queen. I'm really looking forward to seeing you. I've thought about you all weekend and I wanted to tell you that I like everything about you. Your hair, your gorgeous mouth. The way I say "goodbye" and you say "I'm away laughing on a fast camel".

See you Tuesday.

Lots of love,

Robbie.

Phwoar. I put the letter under my pillow. My very first love letter.

1:00 a.m.

Well, unless you count that one that Mark Big Gob sent me, which looked like he had written it with a stick.

1:05 a.m.

Dave the Laugh sent me quite a nice letter when Wet Lindsay deliberately hit me on the ankle with her hockey stick. Actually, the reason I say "I'm away laughing on a fast camel" instead of "goodbye" is because of him.

And "nippy noodles".

1:10 a.m.

And "poo parlour division" instead of "loo".

The Cosmic Horn

Tuesday January 25th

Exhausted, but up like a startled earwig at 8:15 a.m., thanks to Libby blowing her new bugle in my ear. What complete fool has bought her that? Dad, obviously.

School

I wore my beret proudly this morning (not the huge one, as I didn't want to get a reprimand first thing). I wore my beret *à la française* on the side of my head. When I saw Hawkeye, I said, "*Bonjour Madame*, I *aime* a lot your *très bonne* outfit *ce matin.*"

"Just get in to Assembly and try to be normal for once." That's nice, isn't it? You try to add a little bit of beautosity and humorosity into a dull world and that is the thanks you get.

As we slouched past Elvis's hut, I nudged Jas. "Elvis has got a bell! How ludicrously sad is that?" He has a bell on the outside of his hut and a sign above it that says: "Ring the bell for the caretaker". Hahahahahaha.

Assembly

Slim in tip-top jelly form this morning, in her attractive elephant-tent dress. We were all still in *la belle France* mood, saying *"Ah, bonjour"* and nodding at each other a lot and shrugging.

Slim ordered, "Silence, at once. And stop shuffling around like silly geese. I have something very serious to tell you. I am sorry to say that the whole school has been very badly let down by a few bad apples. Girls from this school have been involved in a criminal act. And I intend to make an example of them by punishing them in the severest manner."

All of the Ace Gang looked at each other. God's slippers, what had we done now? Surely Madame Slack hadn't told Slim about the hunchback incident? Or the accidental French flag fiasco?

Hawkeye was glaring at us as we shuffled around. Slim

went on. "Two girls have been arrested for shoplifting in town. Charges are to be made."

All of us went "Yessssss!" (Inwardly). The Bummers had finally come to the end of their reign of terror. Yesss!!!

But then we noticed a dog in the ointment. The Bummers were in the row in front of us, looking as tarty and spotty as normal, and also... not bothered.

Slim continued. "The two girls are Monica Dickens and Pamela Green. They are, as of today, expelled from school. I trust this will be a warning to any girl who imagines that crime has no consequence."

We were all amazed at the news. I kept saying to the others, "Nauseating P. Green? And ADM? Shoplifting?"

Jools said, "Nauseating P. Green can hardly see the end of her nose. She would be a crap shoplifter. She'd have to ask a shop assistant to point things out to her."

She is not wrong.

Weird to think that behind those huge glasses lurked a mistress criminal.

I said, "And ADM?? She came to a school dance in ankle socks once. That is not shoplifting wear."

Break

Behind the sports hall we all huddled together under our coats discussing the scandalosa.

Rosie said, "I can't believe Nauseating P. Green actually went shoplifting in a gang with ADM."

I said, "Do you remember when ADM owned up to Miss Stamp about not having had a shower after games last term? And no one had even noticed that she hadn't. Miss Stamp didn't notice. In fact, I don't think she had actually noticed that ADM had even been doing games. That is not the attitude of a mistress criminal, that is the attitude of an astonishingly dim person. Which is what she is."

"I was never very nice to them," said Jas. I feel bad now. I wonder if we can visit them in jail and maybe take them things... you know, knitted things and so on. Oranges."

I said, "Jas, they are not in the Crimean War. They don't need you to knit balaclavas. They won't go to jail."

Jas was rambling on, "Well, Slim said they were expelled and bad apples and so forth and—"

"Jas, can I say something?"

"What?"

"Shut up."

"Well, I—"

"That is not shutting up, Jas, that is keeping on talking rubbish."

"But..."

We could have kept that up for centuries, but then the Bummers walked around the corner. Jackie Bummer said, "Clear off, tiny tots, we want to have a fag and you are sitting in our ashtray."

Jools (bravely, but stupidly) said, "This is just ground, anyone's ground, it's not..."

Alison came over and got hold of her hair. "You are in our ashtray, so why don't you get out of our ashtray."

We grumbled and groaned as we collected our things. I hate them, I hate them. As the Bummers lit up their fags, Jackie said, "Sad about the criminal element in this school, isn't it?"

In a fit of stupidosity, I said, "Yes, well, why don't you leave, then?" To which Jackie answered, "Careful, Big Nose, as a severe duffing often offends." Then she flicked her cigarette ash on to my head and said, "Oh, whoops."

I had to wash my hair with soap in the loos and then dry it upside down under the hand dryer. Fortunately, I had my mega-duty hair gel with me. Otherwise there would have been a Coco the Clown incident.

Maths

It's a bit funny not having P. Green's head bobbing around at the front of the class. "I miss her," said Rosie. "It's not the same firing elastic bands at no target." She is all heart.

Still, I can't spend any more time thinking about other people. It's only two hours until I meet the Sex God. It's double blodge after this, so providing I don't have to do anything disgusting with pond life, I will be able to get my nails done and foundation on, and possibly mascara, if I crouch down at the back.

Double blodge

I thought of a hilarious biology joke (which is not easy). I wrote to the gang in a gang note: Lockjaw means never having to say you're sorry.

They did their famous cross-eyed sign of approval.

Also, I had a lovely new furry friend (no, not Jas). It's a pickled vole. There are all kinds of disgusting things pickled in jars in the blodge lab, but this is a really cute vole that has its little paws up so that it looks like it is waving at you.

I wave back. I may call it Rover. Rover the vole.

Last bell
In the loos

Mucho excitemondo. My hand was shaking when I was doing my eyeshadow. I very nearly put "sex shimmer" all over my face, which is not attractive. I made Jas wait for me to walk out to the gate. I said, "So, Jazzy Knickers, what are you up to tonight? While I am seeing my boyfriend?"

She was sitting on the sink looking at her sideways reflection. "I've got quite nice cheeks, haven't I?"

"Jas, you've got adorable cheeks. One on each side of your nose. Couldn't be better."

She thought I meant it. "Tom is doing his irrigation project and I'm doing my German homework tonight. It's due in. You should do yours – Herr Kamyer will have a nervy spaz if you don't."

"Jas, as I have said many, many times... never put off until tomorrow what you can avoid altogether."

Jas was still admiring her cheeks. "Well, you say that, but what will you feel like when you go to Germany and you can't say anything?"

"I'm not going to Germany."

"You might, though."

"Well, I won't."

That shut her up for a minute.

"But say you had to."

"Why, what for? I don't like pickled cabbage."

"What if Robbie had to go there for a gig? You'd feel like a *dumschnitzel.*"

Actually she did have a point.

4:20 p.m.

We walked out across the yard to the gates. I made Jas shield me, just in case any of the *Oberführers* were around and noticed that I was all made up. Since the shoplifting fiasco all the staff and prefects are on high alert. Miss Stamp even told Melanie Griffiths off because she didn't have a name tag in her sports knickers. I really, really don't want to imagine how she found that out.

Rosie, Jools and Ellen were loitering without intent near Mr Attwood's hut, so we all linked up. Robbie was leaning on the gate. Phwoar!! I could feel his Sex-Goddy vibes even by Mr Attwood's special bell. But then I noticed that he was not alone, he was talking to Tom and Dave the Laugh and Rollo! Ellen, Jas and Jools nearly fell over with shock. They had no make-up on. Also Ellen had mistakenly put her beret on because she couldn't be arsed to open up her haversack. Emergency, emergency!!!

Ellen snatched off her beret and said, "OhmyGod, ohmyGod, what shall I do??"

In the end Rosie and I formed a sort of defensive wall behind which Ellen and Jas and Jools applied emergency lippy and rolled over their skirts. Rosie and I had to pretend to be swapping books. I was laughing attractively and so was Rosie, as if we were casually unaware that we had three mates crouching behind us. Jas said from near my ankles, "What are they doing? Can they see us?"

"They're just talking."

Rosie said, "We're going to have to pretend to notice them in a minute, are you ready?" Then the three of them leaped up like leaping things and we all walked up to the gates in a state of casualosity (and lip glossiness).

Robbie looked marvy. He gave me his dreamy smile and pushed his hair back. "Hello."

I was in Ditherland. It's bad enough when it's just me and him, but in front of the lads and, in particular, in front of Dave the Laugh, I turned into Herr Kamyer in a skirt (i.e., a twat).

I was completely out-dithered by Ellen, however, who I thought might start doing highland dancing, she was hopping about so much. Tom was nuzzling Jas and she was all red and smiley and dim. How come boys don't go spazoid? They all seemed very cool. I noticed (even though I didn't care) that although Dave the Laugh said hi to Ellen and kissed her cheek, he didn't do any nuzzling. In fact he gave me a look.

It was a "Hello, red-bottomed minx, we meet again"-type look.

My bedroom
9:00 p.m.
I had a dreamy time hanging around with the Sex God. I made all kinds of excuses about wanting to get things from all the shops so that people would see us together. I waved at loads of people, even if I didn't know them very well. I even waved at Mr Across the Road

as he staggered out of the pet shop with two tons of kitty litter. He was so surprised, his bottom nearly dropped off.

Robbie said, "Shopping is over, now it's time for snogging." Then we went and had *le* snog *par excellence* out by the racecourse.

My lips are quite tired, actually. They may have to have an early night.

Midnight

I wonder if Jas is right for once. Maybe Nauseating P. Green will have to go to the naughty girls' prison. Like in *Prisoner: Cell Block H*. She might get duffed up every day by sadists. Much the same as school, really.

Shut up, brain.

I care too much for people. I am a bit like Jesus. Only not so heavily bearded.

Wednesday January 26th
School
On our way to the art room we had a quick burst of "Let's go down the disco" in the corridor until we nearly crashed into

♡

Nauseating P. Green's mum. She was crying as she went into Slim's office.

Oh, poo.

Break

Hiding in the games cupboard. It's full of hockey sticks, but at least it is not minus fifteen degrees like it is outside.

Kate Richardson told me that Jackie Bummer has got ten leather coats, all different colours. And Jackie was also showing off and saying that she and Alison made Nauseating P. Green and ADM go and do their shoplifting for them. Like in *Oliver Twist*... or is it *David Copperfield*? Anyway, one of those really depressing stories about tiny orphans with Fagin in it. They frightened P. Green and ADM into going into shops and putting leather coats on under their own coats and walking out of the shop and then handing them over to the Bummers. They said that if they didn't get six each they would do something horrible to P. Green's hamsters. They even gave them a special tool to get the security labels off.

Rosie said, "Well, why did they get caught, then?"

I explained, "Because P. Green tried to steal six coats at

once. She put them all on under her own coat and then got trapped in the revolving door as she tried to get out."

1:00 a.m.
On the bright side, Mutti says I can have some new boots. To wear to the gig that my boyfriend is playing at on Saturday at the Buddha Lounge.

1:10 a.m.
Did I mention that there is a gig on Saturday that my boyfriend is playing at? Once again I can expose myself as girlfriend of a Sex God? Oo-er.

Thursday January 27th
German
Herr Kamyer was telling us about the Müller family from our German textbook – about Klaus going camping and getting his *kocher* out. Klaus always uses his *kocher to koch* his *spanferkel* (suckling pig). Jas was annoying me by doing a quiz in *Cosmo*. Not an interesting quiz about what kind of skin you have or whether you are a sex bomb or not. It's to find out what your natural body clock is. Whether you

should stay up late, and get up late or whether you should get up early and go to bed early.

Who cares? Jas does. She wrote me a note: *I like to get up early and that makes me a Lark-type person. Tom likes to get up early as well, so he's a Lark and not an Owl, and that makes us get on really well. I wonder what the German for "lark" is?*

I wrote back: Larken. But she doesn't believe me.

I ended up doing the stupid boring quiz because it insinuated itself into my brain. I am very impressionable, which is why people should be very careful about what they bother me with. For instance, when we did *Treasure Island* I developed a limp. Anyway, it turns out that I am a Moderate Owl. On our way to maths I said to Jas, "That means that, although I like to go to bed late and get up late, I am not very fond of fieldmice."

She said, "Your eyes are a bit owly, sort of bulgey."

"Oh dear, now the Little Lark is going to get a duffing from the Moderate Owl." And then I biffed her over the head with my science overall. She said I had to stop, because I was making her fringe go all wonky. And no one wants that.

Break

I have been made hockey captain!!! Honestly, at this rate I will become a regular citizen and possibly start doing voluntary work with the elderly mad! Er no, forget that bit. I've just remembered the last time I went round to Grandad's and accidentally went into his secret money drawer to borrow a few pounds for essentials. Chewing gum and so on. He had set his false teeth open as a trap. When I opened the drawer they slammed shut.

Even though he is supposed to be deaf, Grandad heard his false teeth bang shut from the bottom of his garden. He laughed so much I thought I might have to call the emergency services. But I contented myself by hiding his pipe.

Anyway, back to my triumph on the pitch. Miss Stamp announced that I would be captain. The Ace Gang were all doing "Let's go down the disco" dance as celebration, until Miss Stamp told them to pull themselves together and get into the showers. Which quite literally put a dampener on things...

When we were dressed and going off to English, Miss Stamp took me to one side and said, "You have the makings of quite a good captain, Georgia. Make sure your attitude matches your hockey skills."

I haven't the faintest idea what she is on about. I said to Rosie, "Is she implying that I have insufficient maturiosity?"

Rosie said, "I don't know... but... let's go down the disco!!!!"

We did our special disco inferno dancing across the playing fields. Elvis was lurching around in his overalls. "What are you doing now? Messing about, playing the giddy goat."

I tried to explain pleasantly to the old maniac that we were in girlish high spirits. Pointless, though. He just went mumbling off.

"In my new capacity as hockey captain," I said, "I may have him confined to his hut for the foreseeable future."

In the front room
7:00 p.m.
Vati said, "I'm going to start going to the gym three times a week to get in peak physical condition for our football

matches." I didn't laugh. He started doing a sit-up in the front room. Good grief.

I went off into the kitchen in search of something to eat. Oh yummy, a yoghurt without mould on it! Mum does not take her nurturing role very seriously. But if I complain she'll only say something ridiculous, like, "I'm at work all day. Why don't you make something?"

When I went back into the front room, Dad was back lying on the sofa watching TV. I asked him, "How many sit-ups did you do?"

"Well, I think it's a mistake to rush into things."

"Just the one, then?"

He pretended to be interested in some gardening programme.

7:30 p.m.

Mum came in from her girls' aerobics all red and giddy. She said to Vati, "Don't get up, Bob, try and rest yourself." But I don't think she meant it. I followed her into the kitchen in the hope that she might have some food hidden in her leotard. She did have a tin of beans, as it happens, so we tucked in.

"It's very very like Paris in our home," I told her.

She wasn't paying any attention – just being red and adjusting her bra. Then she burbled on. "We had such a laugh tonight, Gee. Prue and Sandy went to this singles bar the other night and got off with a couple of Russian sailors. Sandy said Ivan could only say *"Niet"* but that he was a really good snogger."

I just looked at her.

"Mum, that is disgusting."

"Why?"

"Because, well, they are mothers."

"I know, but they haven't got husbands any more. They are single women again who have children."

"I know, but..."

She'd gone off on one, though. "Do you think that anyone over twenty-five should just stay in for ever?"

"Yes."

"You're being ridiculous."

"I am not."

"You're a teenage prude."

I was thinking, "A prude, am I? You wouldn't say that if you knew the amount of lip nibbling I had done. I have been practically eaten alive by boys!!" But I didn't say it.

8:30 p.m.
In the bath, contemplating my life as the girlfriend of a Sex God and also tip-top hockey captain.

And also why nunga-nungas float. What is the point of that? Perhaps in prehistoric days they were used as lifebelts in times of flood. But if that was the case, why did they bother with Noah's Ark? Mrs Noah and all the women could have just floated about and everyone else could have climbed on board.

Then I heard raised voices. Libby started shouting, "Fight, fight!!"

Vati was yelling. "I don't watch television all the time... and what if I did, what's wrong with that?"

Mum yelled back. "It's boring – that's what's wrong with it!"

"Well let's talk about bloody aerobics, then. Go on, tell me how many times you wiggled your arse in time to the music!"

"Boring pig!"

And then Libby started yelling, "Bad piggy, bad piggy!!"

Sacré bloody *bleu*. I am going to be an orphan soon. Ah well.

Friday January 28th
Breakfast

This not talking to each other thing is driving me to the brink of bonkerosity. How am I supposed to experience growing up if the so-called grown-ups are making *me* be the most grown-up?

Mum said to me, "Would you ask your father if he would mind looking after his daughter Liberty tomorrow evening, as I have a pressing social engagement?"

Oh, good Lord. I said to Dad, who was half an inch away fiddling with his beard, "Dad, would you mind looking after your daughter Liberty tomorrow evening, which is, incidentally, when I shall be at a pressing social engagement myself, because Mutti also has a pressing social engagement, apparently."

Dad went all red and trousery. He said, "This is ballocks."

I said to Mum, "He said this is ballocks."

And Dad said, "Don't bloody swear. It's not clever."

And I said, "And he said, don't bloody swear it's not clever."

Dad started to say, "Don't be so bl—" and then he stopped and I looked at him in a helpful way and said, "And he said, don't be so bl—" But he walked out and slammed the door.

Mum said, "He's so childish." Which is true, but I think it's ironic that she should say it when she is wearing a T-shirt that says "Go girl" and fluffy mules.

Saturday January 29th

Up at the crack of 8:00 a.m. for pre-gig preparation.

Vati was up as well in his ludicrous football shorts. He was being all "masculine". Mum was still ignoring him, but I said, "Goodbye, Vati, this may be the last time I see you fully limbed."

He chucked me under my chin(!) and said, "I'm in my prime, Georgia, they won't know what hit them." Then he strode off like he thought he was David Beckham. Which I think he does.

I said to Mum, "Vati is very very like David Beckham, isn't he? Apart from being porky, heavily bearded and crap at football."

She just tutted and did that basooma adjusting thing she does.

10:00 a.m.

When I came out of the bathroom wrapped in a towel Mum was staring at me. Sort of inspecting me. Surely she couldn't tell that I had used her strictly forbidden skin stuff?

"What?" I said.

"Your elbows stick out a lot."

What??? What fresh hell? Sticky-out elbows??? I said, "What are you talking about?"

She was prodding my arms. "Well they do, don't they? I've never noticed them sticking out like that before. Look at mine. They aren't like yours. Do you think you've dislocated them playing hockey or something?"

Dislocated my elbows? I stormed off to my room to inspect them. Perfectly ordinary elbows. Maybe a bit sticky-outy, though.

Phoned Jas. "Jas, do you think my elbows stick out?"

She was, as usual, chewing something, probably her fringe. "They've always been a bit odd-looking."

Thank you, Nurse Jas. She's too self-obsessed to bother

with my elbows. She just raved on about how she and Tom have joined The Ramblers' Association. She's not kidding. She could ramble on for England. I didn't know there was a special association for it.

Lunchtime
In my bedroom
I am having some relaxing "me" time. And "me" time means groovy music and an eye mask. Libby is making some ear-muffs for the kittykats, out of some cottonwool, I think.

1:30 p.m.
Mum came in and went ballisticisimus. The cottonwool ear-muffs for the kittykats are made from her new packet of tampons. She huffed off with what was left and accused me of selfishosity for not noticing. I yelled after her, "Mum, it is very hard to notice anything when you have tea bags on your eyes."

She came back in again to take Libby down for her bath and said, "I think we should get those elbows looked at."

What is she rambling on about? Get them looked at by whom? An elbowologist, no doubt. On the funny side, I have just looked up "elbow" in German and it is *Ellbogen*.

Campingfahrt means not, as you might imagine, an unfortunate incident with Libby in a tent... it means "camping trip". I think I have a natural talent for languages.

6:30 p.m.
Mucho excitemondo and jelly knickers activity. I am a vision in black, wearing my new and groovoid boots.

7:00 p.m.
Met the gang at the usual place to go to the gig. Sven had his special flares on. They have a battery in them and little lightbulbs all the way down the seams. When he presses the battery his trousers light up. He really is bonkers. And huge.

When we got to the door of the Buddha Lounge he said to the door guy, "Got evening, I am Sven and these are my chicks. Let us in, my trousers want to boogie." And Rosie isn't a bit embarrassed.

We all went immediately to the loos. It was the usual scrum in there. Ellen was sooooo nervous (again), like a jellybean on a trampoline. She kept going into a ditherspaz saying, "I really, really rate Dave, you know."

We said, "We know."

"But I really, you know, like him."

"WE KNOW!!!"

Out in the club it was heaving. We found a little corner to use as gang headquarters and had a good eyeball around. All the lads were by the bar, Dave the L (hmmm, cool shirt), Rollo, Tom and a bunch of their friends. Oh, and Mark Big Gob was there with his rough mates. I hadn't seen him since the telephone box incident. He deliberately looked at my nungas and licked his lips. How disgusting he is!!! I pity his poor tiny midget girlfriend. At least my basoomas are nicely protected in their Christmas holder. Mutti said she got it specially because it had "extra-firm control".

Then, from behind the stage, The Stiff Dylans came out to start their set. Groovy pyjamas. Everyone went wild. The Sex God looked around and saw me (just casually flicking my hair back and exuding sophisticosity). He smiled at me and then blew me a kiss. Oh, yes! In front of everyone. Oh, yes and *bon*!"

10:00 p.m.

Dancefest *extraordinaire*. Top fun all night. As I may have said before, Dave the Laugh is... er... a laugh. And also quite a cool dancer. Ellen doesn't really like dancing, so when she had gone off to the ladies' he made me do the conga with him. He made me do it to "Oh No, It's Me Again", which is one the Sex God composed that's on my Chrimbo compilation tape. It's a slow number and really serious about someone (Van Gogh, I think) who wakes up and looks at himself in the mirror and says, "Oh no, it's me again," which is depressing. But not to Dave the Laugh, who thought it was a conga opportunity. Robbie was singing with his eyes closed (hmmm, very moody), but then during the slow guitar break he looked up and I think he caught sight of me and Dave conga dancing. He didn't look full of happinosity. In fact, he looked a bit miffed.

I stopped doing the conga then, but Dave shouted at me, "Don't stop mid-conga; it's very bad for my cong."

What in the name of Elton John's codpiece is he on about? He's naughty, though. When we were dancing he let his hands sort of drift on to my bottom. I could feel it slightly flushing. Down, bottom, down.

Ellen still wasn't back from the loo, so we went across to the bar to get a cold drink. He said, "I think I have got the General Horn."

I said, "What is that?"

He explained that "having the horn" means fancying people. And it's got various stages. "You can have Specific Horn, when you fancy one person. Then if it gets worse you get the General Horn, which is when you fancy loads of people. But worst of all is the Cosmic Horn."

He was really making me laugh and feel funny at the same time, but I couldn't help asking, "What in the name of Lucifer's bottom is the Cosmic Horn?"

"That is when you fancy everything and everyone in the universe."

Blimey.

Ellen came over then and grabbed Dave's arm. She said, all girlie, "Dave, do you fancy going outside? I'm a bit hot."

Dave sort of hesitated and looked at me in a peculiar way and then said, "Me too." And they went off. Ellen is sooo keen on him, it's ridiculous.

I said to Jas (and Tom, as they are like Siamese twins. I wonder what happens when she goes to the loo?),

"Honestly, Ellen is really uncool about Dave. She practically stalks him."

Jas said, "You stalked Robbie."

I laughed in an attractive way. "Oh Jas, I did not stalk him..."

Jas rambled on like an unstoppable loon. "And you made me assistant stalker. Also, do you remember when you made me go round to Wet Lindsay's house and we went and looked in her bedroom window and saw her in her thong?"

Tom said, "You went round to Lindsay's house and looked in her window? I didn't know that! Does Robbie know?"

I quickly said, "Tom, have you ever had the Cosmic Horn?"

Just then The Stiff Dylans finished their set and came off stage. I went off to find Robbie for the snog break, but it was hopeless. There were loads of girls all crowded around him in the dressing room, and I couldn't get near.

He said over the top of their heads, "I'll walk you home at the end, don't leave."

Midnight
Outside the Buddha Lounge, Jas asked, "Is your vati picking you up?"

"No," I told her. "I've got a special prison pass, which means that I am allowed to get home by myself. Mostly because Mum is out and Dad can't walk after playing football with the "lads". They only lost by 13–0."

The gang set off, a band of merry snoggers and I was left outside by myself.

12:15 a.m.
Brr, quite nippy noodles. Where is he?

I went and looked in through the doors. Robbie was talking to six girls; the rest of the band's girlfriends, Sam, Mia and India, and another three. I recognised a couple of them because they used to be in the sixth form and had gone off to London to fashion college or something. Perhaps that explained why one (Petra) was wearing a Tibetan bonnet with ear-flaps. Petra had long blonde hair that poked out of her bonnet (very Tibetan... not). She was swishing it about like, er, a swishing thing. Robbie was laughing with them. But as I always say, "She who laughs last... er... doesn't always get the joke."

Why was he talking to them? Perhaps he was doing PR for his career. Or perhaps they were like those groupies I read about that used to hang around boys in groups and make little statues of their manly parts out of plaster of Paris. I didn't see any bags of plaster, though. Although one of them did have a haversack. The plaster might be in there. Just then Robbie saw me and said, "Georgia, hi."

Petra looked round and said (in a bonnetty way), "Oh hi, Georgia. Long time no dig. How are you? How's Stalag 14? Not wearing your beret?" And she laughed in a common way.

Robbie looked a bit uncomfortable and said quite quickly, "Well, nice to see you all again, see you later. Come on, Georgia."

Hahahaha and double hahaha. That shut Petra up. She looked amazed to see me and Robbie walk off together.

Robbie was a bit quiet on the way home, but when we walked through the park he got hold of me and kissed me for a really long time. I only remembered to start breathing half way through, so nearly passed out.

It was like a snoggers' rave in the park. Every bush was full of them. Mark Big Gob was there with his tiny little girlfriend. And it was very dark, but I am almost sure that he picked her up and put her on a tree stump to snog her.

Either that or her legs get very fat towards the ankles.

When we got to my gate, Robbie said, "Petra and Kate have just come back from backpacking round India and Nepal."

I said, "Oh, that explains the ear-flaps."

The Sex God pinched my nose. "What am I going to do with you?"

"Take me to Hamburger-a-gogo land with you."

"Hmm, I wonder what your dad would say to that."

"He'd say bye and God bless all who sail in you." SG didn't look like he believed me. Or knew what in the name of arse I was talking about.

1:00 a.m.

Libby was still up when I got in. She had her pyjama top on but her bottom was flowing free and wild. She is not what you would call inhibited, which is a pity. She was giving Teddy a late-night haircut. Mum said when I came in, "Come on, Libbs, it's very late and your big sister is home now. Time for bed."

Libby didn't even look up, she just said, in an alarmingly grown-up voice, "Not now, dear, I'm busy."

2:00 a.m.

Kissed the back of my hand goodnight. I think I am becoming a champion snogger. As Peter Dyer said when I went for snogging lessons, I apply just the right sort of pressure, not too pressing and not too giving. Much like my nature, I like to think.

In a way, it's a shame not to share my special snogging talents far and wide.

3:00 a.m.

What am I talking about? I love the Sex God, end of bottom. I mean end of story.

3:15 a.m.

Looked out my window. Angus and Naomi are on the wall... Do cats snog? Perhaps they have a cat snogging scale.

3:30 a.m.

Do owls snog?

SHUT UP, SHUT UP. This is all Dave the Laugh's fault with his Cosmic Horn talk.

Monday January 31st

Met Jas at her gate. She showed me her Ramblers' Association badge. Honestly. Apparently you go off with other half-wits and wander around the countryside looking at things. I said to her, "The gig was groovy bananas, wasn't it?"

"Yeah, fabby."

"Jas, don't you ever, you know... get the horn for anyone else besides Tom?"

"No. I am not like you. Promiscuous."

"Jas, I'm not promiscuous."

"Well, you flirt with Dave the Laugh."

"Well, I—"

"In fact, you snog Dave the Laugh... and I bet you would snog Gorgey Henri if he asked you."

"Well... I..." For once she had a sort of point.

The Ace Gang all wore enormous berets this morning to remind us of our visit to *la belle France*. It seems about six hundred years ago. We have decided to commemorate the occasion by having a National Hunchback Day. Maybe we will wait till things cool down a bit at Stalag 14 first, though.

♡ 175

When we got near the school gates we took the comedy berets off and had our ordinary ones underneath. (From comedy to tragedy in one movement!) So hahahaha to the *Oberführers*. We are too full of cleverosity for them.

As we were walking past Hawkeye something really horriblimus happened. Nauseating P. Green was standing near the gates! She looked like she had been blubbing for about a million years. I smiled at her and she started to come over to us. Oh, good grief. Then Hawkeye saw her and said, "Pamela Green, you are not to come anywhere near this school again. You are a complete disgrace."

P. Green started blinking and stuttering. "But Mrs Heaton, I... I didn't... it wasn't me, I..."

Hawkeye just snapped at us. "Come on, you girls, get into school NOW!" I wonder if she was a doberman in a previous life.

Cloakroom

I said to Jas, "Nauseating P. Green is obviously a twat of the first water but I do feel sorry for her."

Jas said, "I wonder if we should... er... go and see someone about it."

Rosie said, "And then get the duffing-up of a lifetime from the Bummers?"

Hmm, she had a point.

Still.

Games

Brrrrrrrrrrrrr. Miss Stamp has had us doing hockey manoeuvres in minus five hundred and forty.

As we shivered I said to Jas, "Even seals would stay in their little seal homes on days like this. They would stay snuggly tucked up knitting and chatting."

Jas got interested in the seals. She's a bit obsessed with sea creatures, I think. "Do you think they have their own language? I wonder what sort of thing they talk about?"

"They talk about the great seal package holidays they had been on. Greenland by night, Antarctica weekend breaks, two nights on a top-class iceberg and as much krill as you can eat."

This is the life. Charging around on a frozen pitch, whacking concrete balls at each other with sticks. Once you got the feeling back in your bum it was quite good fun, actually. I was tearing up and down the pitch like David Beckham (without the shaved head and manly parts, of course, but with the consummate ball skills). Well, until I accidentally whacked Jas on the knee (above the shin pad) with a ball.

It was her fault, really. I whacked a really good goal in the net but Mrs Slow Knickers didn't get out of the way in time (probably because she was weighed down by her enormous sports pantibus). As she hobbled off she was moaning and groaning and blaming me. "You're mad, Georgia, hitting balls around like... like..."

I said, helpfully, "Like a brilliant hockey captain?"

"No, not like that."

"Well, like what?"

She was red as a loon. I gave her my famous world-renowned affectionate hug, but she pushed me off and said "Like... a promiscuous HOOLIGAN."

Oooooooh. Now she had really upset me.

Lunchtime

Lad alert!!! Lad alert!!! Dave the Laugh was at the school gates. He looked in a bit of a funny mood. Normally he is all smiley and sort of cocky (oo-er), but he wasn't smiling. And he looked a bit tense. He is really nice-looking. If I didn't have the Sex God I would definitely want to go out with him. Especially as Tom told me that Dave made a huge banner and hung it on top of their school, and it said, "For sale". Which anyone can see is vair vair funny. By the time I got to gang headquarters (first floor loos), Ellen was being Dithering Queen *extraordinaire*. She was saying, "Oh, oh, what shall I do? What shall I do?"

Jas said, "Just go and talk to him. He's come to see you. That's really nice." Then she went all dreamy and dim. "Tom sometimes just gets an urge to see me and he comes to meet me on the—"

I said, "Veggie van?"

She didn't even look at me. She just continued to talk to Ellen as if I hadn't said anything vair vair hilarious. "He comes to see me on the spur of the moment." Then she gave me her worst look (scary bananas) and limped off.

I called after her, "You know I love you, Jas. Why are you not touching me with a barge pole? And eschewing me with a firm hand? And *ignorez-vousing* me?" She still didn't pay any attention.

After about a million years applying lip gloss, Ellen went out to meet Dave the L.

We all watched from the loo windows while they talked. I said to Jools, "He didn't snog her when he saw her, did he?"

Rosie was doing her toenails; she had bits of soap in between each toe to stop the polish going smeary. I must remember not to use the soap ever again.

Anyway, Rosie said, "Sven always snogs me when he first sees me. In fact he snogs me pretty much all the time. Even when he is eating."

We all said, "Erlack!"

Dave and Ellen went behind the bike shed and we couldn't see what was happening. I was sort of glad about that somehow, because even though I had a boyfriend, was ecstatic, in seventh heaven, couldn't be happier, never thought about another boy for a second, had set aside my red bottom with a firm hand, only had the Specific Horn with no sign of the General Horn at all, I didn't really like to see Dave the Laugh snogging other people. I don't know why.

Maths

Ellen was blubbing in maths. She was sniffling next to Jas and I could see that she was telling her what had happened, but as Jas is even *ignorez-vousing* my notes, I couldn't find out anything. Then Ellen put her hand up and said she felt ill and could she go to sick bay.

I know I often feel like blubbing during maths, but I thought she was being a bit over the top having to go to sick bay. Mind you we were doing pi, and I may have said this many times before, but didn't the ancient Greeks have anything better to do than measure things? Or leap out of baths, yelling "*Eureka!*"

When Miss Stamp (quarter lesbian, quarter sports *Oberführer* and also quarter maths teacher... hang on, that only makes her a three-quarter person... ah well) asked us why Archimedes shouted "*Eureka!*" when his bath overflowed, I said it was because eureka is Greek for "Bloody hell, this bath is hot!!!" Which may well be the first ancient Greek joke.

Afternoon break

World news breaking! Dave has dumped Ellen!! And Ellen is not a happy dumpee. In the chemistry lab loos Ellen was nearly hysterical. Her eyes were all swollen like mice eyes. She was gulping and trying to talk, and then blubbing again.

Nurse Jas was hugging her.

Finally Ellen managed to say, "He, he, said he first realised at the... at the... fish party that he... that he... that he..." Sniffle, sniffle, gulp.

I thought, I'm ever so peckish. I wonder if it would be really unfeeling if I just nibbled on my Mars bar.

But then Ellen managed to go on. "I mean, I said to him... 'Is it something I've done?' And he said... he said... 'No, you're a great girl, it's something I've done, not you. It's a sort of General Horn-type thing.' What does he mean?? What has he done? What General Horn thing?"

Oh God. Oh Goddy God God.

The others were nodding, but Jas was nodding and looking at me. Like a wise old owl in a skirt. But with arms instead of wings. And no beak.

Then the bell went. Phew.

4:30 p.m.

On the way home, Jas walked really quickly ahead of me, like she had something stuck up her bottom. I nearly had to jog to get alongside her. I put my arm around her and she sped up even more, so that we were both jogging along.

I said, "Jas, Jas, my little pal, I'm sorry about bonking you on your knee. Do you want me to kiss it? Or carry you home? I will. I will do anything if you will be my little pal again."

Jas stopped. "All right, don't drop me, though." So I had to carry her home. All the way home. And she is not light – her knickers alone must weigh about half a stone.

I was nearly dead by the time we reached her gate. I tried to put her down, but she said, "This is the gate, not my bed." So I had to carry her right to the door. She unlocked the door still in my arms, while my head practically fell off with redness, and then I had to carry her upstairs to her bedroom.

It did make us laugh, though. As we were lying on her bed with a squillion of her soft toys, I said, "Jas, have you forgiven me now?"

"Polish my Ramblers' badge." So I had to polish the badge. Then she said, "I might be preparing myself to forgive you."

I fed her a cheesy Wotsit and she munched on it. Then she said, "But will Ellen forgive you?"

"What do you mean? For what?"

"For snogging her boyfriend and; for... for allowing your red bottom to rule the roost."

"Jas, my bottom is not a chicken."

"You know what I mean."

"Don't start all that 'you know what I mean' business."

"Yes, but you do know what I mean."

My room

Jas thinks that I should tell Ellen what happened *vis-à-vis* Dave the Laugh, because then she will know that he is a serial snogger and lip nibbler... or whatever... and then she will not pine for him.

Hmmm. She might not pine for him, but she might pull my head off.

Mum came bustling in. "Are you ready?"

"For what? Nuclear war? World peace? Tea? A surprise inheritance?"

"Dr Clooney... er, I mean Dr Gilhooley."

"Gorgey though he is, Mum, why would I be ready for him?"

5:00 p.m.

I had a quick look at my *Ellbogen*. I haven't thought about them much lately because of all the other emergencies that have been happening. They are a bit odd-looking, actually, when you get them naked. And I won't be able to go around wearing long sleeves for the rest of my life, especially in California. And what about the press when I go to premieres and stuff with Robbie? I don't want headlines pointing my elbows out to the world: *"Sex God and weird girl with sticky-out elbows go to top restaurant."*

As we entered the Valley of the Unwell (Dr Clooney's waiting room), I said to Mum quietly, "What can he do about them anyway?" I said it quietly because the room was, as usual, full of the mentally deranged.

Dr Clooney is quite gorgeous. Blue-eyed, dark and sort of sexy. He makes Mum go in a terrible tizz, all flushed and basoomy. He said, "How can I help?"

Mum pulled up my sleeves exposing my elbows and said, "Her elbows stick out."

Dr Clooney laughed for about a million years. He said, "Honestly, I would pay you two girls to come to my surgery every day." Then he walked over to examine my elbows.

Dr Clooney smiled at me. Phwoar!! "Georgia is a racehorse."

What in the name of Miss Stamp's moustache and

matching eyebrows is he talking about?

He went on. "She's got long limbs and not much fat on her body, so her elbows seem to be more boney and exposed than someone who has a different body shape. As she grows they'll be less noticeable."

I thought Mum was going to snog him on the spot. "Oh, thank you, Doctor, it was such a worry. Anyway, how have you been doing? Done any dancing lately?"

On the way home I said to Mum, "What did you mean, done any dancing lately?"

Mum went all red and delirious. "Well, I've just, you know, seen him out sometimes, when I've been with the girls... dancing, and..."

"Yes... and...?"

"Well, he's very fit." Oh, dear God. My own mother is displaying alarming signs of the General Horn.

9:00 p.m.

On the plus side, the *Ellbogen* mystery is solved... I am a racehorse.

10:00 p.m.

Rosie phoned. "Georgia. Something really awful has happened."

"Has your hair gone all sticky up? I think mine has."

"No, it's not that."

"Lurker alert?"

"No, worse."

"Blimey. You're not having a baby Sven, are you?"

"Sven is being sent back to Swedenland. He has to help out with his family farm, or whatever they have over there."

"Is it a reindeer farm?"

"GEORGIA, I DON'T KNOW and I don't care!!!"

Rosie is sheer desperadoes. She says if Sven goes to Swedenland, she goes too. I said, "Well you'd better find out where it is first. You drew the wheat belt across the Irish Sea in our last geoggers test."

Tuesday February 1st
Breakfast
8:05 a.m.

This is ridiculous – Mum and Dad are still not speaking. Normally I would be glad of the silence, except it means they both speak to me and ask me things. Like, "So, what's number one this week in the pop charts?" How sad is that?

School

It's like the Valley of the Damned. Rosie is moping around, Jools has had a fight with Rollo and Ellen is sniffling around the place like a sniffler *extraordinaire*. You only have to say to her, "Do you fancy one of my cheesy Wotsits?" and she runs off to the loos blubbing. And Jas keeps looking at me. Looking and looking.

I said to her, "You should be careful, Jas, one of the first formers was in a staring competition last week and she stared for so long that her eyes went dry and she had to go to hospital to have them watered."

She just sniffed. It is a very very good job that I am full of cheeriosity, also a tip-top hockey captain.

RE

Rosie sent me a note: I've found out where Swedenland is. I'm going to go after Sven and get a job and make new Sweden-type friends.

I wrote back: Is there much call for fifteen-year-old snoggers in Swedenland?

She looked at me when she got the note and did her famous impression of a cross-eyed loon. Then she wrote: Anyway, what will YOU do in Hamburger-a-gogo land for a job? Your very amusing impression of a lockjaw germ, or... er... that's it.

Evening

Same bat time. Same bat place.

Libby was applying some of Mutti's face powder and lipstick to Angus while he sat on my bed. And he didn't seem to mind. In fact, he was purring. Becoming a furry vati has made him alarmingly mellow. Or a homosexualist.

Robbie has gone off for some interview thing. He didn't really explain what it was about. Popstar stuff, I suppose. Rosie is very very wrong if she thinks I will not be able to do anything in Hamburger-a-gogo land. I could form a girlfriends' hockey 11 and play my way across America.

Wednesday February 2nd

Hockey tournament today with me at the helm. But more to the point, Wet Lindsay has resigned from the team.

HURRAH! She says it is a protest against me being hockey captain, because I am a facsimile of a sham and have the attitude of a juvenile pea. Useless stick insect ankle molester.

6:30 p.m.
Cracking victory!!! The most amazing day. We played six matches and won all six! I scored in each match, and even though I do say it myself... I AM A HOCKEY GENIUS!!!

I had to give a speech when I accepted the cup for our school. It was my chance to show the world and, in particular, the heavily moustachioed Miss Stamp that I am full of wisdomosity and maturiosity and *gravitas* (not gravy ass, as Rosie thought). I said, "I would just like to say that I owe this victory to many people. To my team, to my school, to my mum and dad for having me, to the ancient Britons for giving me my proud heritage, to the early cavemen, without whom none of us would have got here, as they invented the wheel..."

Miss Stamp was about to implode but she couldn't do anything because the head of All Saints school seemed to think I was being *très amusant* and clapped A LOT at the end of my speech.

Thursday February 3rd
School

Hahahahaha. Slim had to mention my name in assembly and congratulate me!!!

Hawkeye looked like she had poo in her mouth (which she probably did). Slim, as usual, was in a ludicrously bad mood. Her chins were trembling in time to the hymns. She said, "Despite what I have said before, certain elements in this school continue to think they can carry on flouting school rules. Mr Attwood misplaced his cap a day or two ago and found it today, burnt to a cinder. This is my final warning to you all: be very, very careful of your behaviour, as all misdemeanours will be treated very seriously."

As we ambled off to English, I said, "Mr Attwood probably set fire to his own hat on purpose. He hates us because we are young and lively."

Jas said, "And because we drop skeletons on him."

"Well, yes—"

"And the locusts ate his overalls..."

"Yes, well there is—"

"And he tripped over his—"

"Jas, shut up."

RE

Rosie has been living in Glum City all day since her beloved Sven got in his Viking boat (Olau Lines ferry) and went off to Swedenland today. He has only gone for one month, but she insists that she is going to go and live in Swedenland with him for that month. Miss Wilson was telling us about her unhappy childhood, so I took the opportunity to draw some fashion items for Rosie to take with her to the Nordic wastes. I drew her wearing furry glasses and a nose warmer. I even did a vair vair funny drawing of her in a fur bikini, but she could hardly be bothered to join in, even when we started our traditional RE humming. (We all start humming really softly and at the same time carry on as normal so that you can't tell we are humming. Or where the humming is coming from.) Miss Wilson thought it might be the radiators. It drives Miss Wilson round the proverbial bend... not so far to go in her case.

Break

In sheer desperadoes to cheer Rosie up, I had a moment of my usual geniosity. We were slouching along past Elvis's hut with its stupid sign that says: "Ring the bell for the caretaker." I said to Ro Ro, "*Un moment, mon* pally." Then I went and rang his bell.

He came looning to his door, like the grumpiest, most mad man in the universe, which he is. He glared at me and then said, "What do you want?"

I said, pointing to his sign, "What I want to know, Mr Attwood, is why you can't ring your own bell."

Anyway, he didn't get it. He was rambling on and I was just about to slope politely off, when Wet Lindsay came round the corner. She was ogling us like an ogler with stick legs, which she is.

Elvis was so red I thought his head might explode, but sadly, it didn't. He was shouting, "It's always you, messing about, coming in my hut. You let those bloody locusts eat my spare overalls..."

I tried to be reasonable with the old maniac. "Mr Attwood, Elvis, I wasn't to know that the locusts would eat your overalls. I merely thought they would like a little fly around in the blodge lab after being cooped up in their cage."

Mr Attwood was still yelling. "...and I bet it was you who burnt my cap!"

Oh, for heaven's sake.

Maths

I was just peacefully buffing my half-moons, when Hawkeye put her head round the door. She barked, "My office, now!!!"

Hawkeye's office

Oh sacré bloody bleu. Hawkeye was livid as a loon. She was all rigid with indignosity. "I am sick to death of this, Georgia Nicolson. You have a perfectly good brain and a few talents, and you INSIST on squandering them in silly, childish pranks and unkindnesses. When Miss Stamp told me that she had chosen you as hockey captain, I had grave doubts. I still sometimes get headaches from your ridiculous display at the tennis championships last year."

Oh Blimey O'Reilly's vest and pants, what is it with teachers? Do they make lists of things that happened ages and ages ago and just hang around waiting for something else to add to them? Why doesn't she read some of the books I read? Let things go... relax, don't sweat the small stuff, talk to dolphins, go with the flow... etc.

Hawkeye hadn't finished. "However, these latest so-called jokes have confirmed what I said to her: that you have a silly attitude and are a poor example to both your peers and, more especially, the young and impressionable girls in this school. You are relieved of your duties as hockey captain forthwith."

I started to try to say something, but I felt a funny prickling feeling in my throat. I had to hand back my captain's badge. And what is more, I am on gardening duty with Mr Attwood for a month!

When I came out of Hawkeye's interrogation room, Wet Lindsay was smirking around. I bet she snitched on me. I didn't dignify her by saying anything. I have more pridosity than that.

Rosie was waiting for me around the corner. "Was it the forty lashes or has she just cut your basoomas off as a warning to others?"

"She's sacked me from being hockey captain."

Ro Ro put her arm around me.

My bedroom
11:17 p.m.
I wanted to phone the Sex God and tell him about the hockey captain fiasco and I was going to. But I wasn't sure

whether he would think that the "Ring the bell for the caretaker" thing was *trés amusant* or the act of a twat.

Midnight
I bet Dave the Laugh would think it was... er... a laugh.

Why am I thinking about him?

Friday February 4th
Lunchtime
I didn't feel much like talking and the gang kept being nice to me, which was a bit strange. So I went off by myself to think. What was it Billy Shakespeare said? "And as we walk on down the road, our shadow taller than our souls..." Oh no, that was Rolf Harris doing his version of "Stairway to Heaven".

How crap was that?

The gang were following me around at a distance. Like stalkers in school uniforms.

I really loved being captain, though. Oh, double poo.

Even when you are the girlfriend of a Sex God things can go wrong. And anyway, what is the point of being the girlfriend of someone if every time you want to tell him something you can't? That is like being the ungirlfriend of someone. That is what I am: an ungirlfriend.

And not hockey captain. And with quite sticky-out elbows.

I moped around to the back of the tennis courts and a voice shouted out, "Has naughty Big Nose been in trouble with the scary teacher?" The Bummers were sitting having a fag on a pile of coats.

Oh, joy. The *pièce de résistance. Merde*, poo and triple bum.

Alison Bummer had a draw on her fag and then went off into a sort of hacking coughing fit.

I said, "Still in tip-top physical condition then, Alison, I'm pleased to see."

Alison gave me a very unattractive look (which is actually the only look she has). And I was just walking off when I heard a little voice say, "Can I get out now? It's almost end of break and my knees are really hurting."

Jackie said, "I'd like to let you out, but I haven't finished my fag yet." And I realised the Bummers had some poor little first formers underneath the coats on "chair duty".

I turned back. "Let them out, you two."

Jackie pretended to be really scared. "Oh, OK then, Georgia, because we are sooooooo very very frightened of you."

Alison joined in. "Yes, you might hurt us with your enormous nose."

I looked at them and I thought, *Right, that is it. I have been pushed to the brink of my tether. My hockey career might be over, but there is still something I can do for England.* (And no I did not mean leave it.)

I marched back so quickly to school that the stalkers had to almost run to keep up with me.

They did catch me just as I was going into Slim's outer sanctum. "Gee, what are you doing?" Jas asked.

I said, "I'm going to tell Slim about Nauseating P. Green and the Bummers."

Everyone said, "OhmyGod!!!"

Jools said, "They will kill you if they find out."

Rosie said, "Slim might not trust you because of all the trouble you've been in."

I said, with great dignosity, "I will have to take my chance, then."

Then this really weird thing happened. Jas said, "I'm going to come in with you and tell what I know as well." So

I hugged her. She tried to get away from me and spoiled the moment by saying, "Well... you know... erm... I mean, I am a member of the Ramblers' Association and..."

She would have rambled on, but Rosie said, "Yes, I'll come in as well. I will be on a reindeer farm by summer anyway, so what do I have to lose?"

All the Ace Gang said they would come to tell Slim with me. Even Ellen stopped sniffling long enough to join us. We were like the Six Samurai or whatever it is. We could ride around the countryside wronging rights and so on.

Then Slim appeared like a wardrobe in a dress and I slightly changed my mind.

4:30 p.m.
Well, we did it. We snitched on the Bummers and they have been immediately suspended from school and the police went straight round to their houses. God knows what will happen next.

6:00 p.m.
I'll tell you what happened next. Nauseating P. Green and her mum came round to my house. OhmyGod, they know

where I live!!! They were blubbing and carrying on in an alarming way.

Nauseating P. Green brought Hammy her hamster around to celebrate, which was a bit of a mistake because Angus took him off to play hide and seek with Naomi and the kids. But we managed to find Hammy in the end and I think his fur may grow back in time.

The P. Greens left after several centuries of excruciating boredom and goldfishiness. But sadly it didn't end there. I have become a heroine in my own lunchtime.

Vati said, "I am really, really proud of you, my love." I thought he was going to start blubbing.

Mum was hugging me. In fact, they both forgot they were not speaking to each other and they were BOTH hugging me. Then Libby joined in with Teddy and scuba-diving Barbie. I never thought the day would dawn when I would be the victim of a group hug.

I may never do another nice thing in my life – it really isn't worth it.

9:00 p.m.
Robbie rang. I started to tell him about my day. "Hi Robbie,

honestly, WHAT a day I've had. Well, guess what happened. The Bummers were sitting on some first formers and—"

Robbie interrupted me. "Georgia, look, I have to see you tomorrow, it's quite serious."

I said, "Have you broken a plectrum?"

But he didn't laugh.

Midnight

Oh God. What now? What fresh hell?

Go forth, Georgia, and use your red bottom wisely

Saturday February 5th

I am meeting the Sex God at the bottom of the clock tower. Libby wanted to come with me and ran off with my make-up bag. She ran in to the bathroom and held my bag over the loo, saying, "Me come."

I had no time to negotiate, so... I just lied. "OK, go and get your welligogs on."

She ambled off to get them and I snatched my make-up bag and escaped through the door. There will be hell to pay when I get home. In fact, I will be surprised if there is a home left by the time I get back.

I had to apply my make-up crouching behind our garden wall. I could see Mr Across the Road looking at me. He should do some voluntary work – perhaps he could be a seeing-eye dog or something.

11:00 a.m.

Robbie was already at the clock tower when I got there. As soon as I arrived he pulled me to him, which was a bit of a shame as he was wearing a coat with quite big buttons and one went right up my nose. I didn't say anything, though.

He said, "Let's walk to the park. I want to go to that place where we first sat together. Do you remember?"

Oooh, how *romantico*. He sang his first song to me there with my head on his knees. (He was sitting down at the time, otherwise I would have looked ridiculous.)

On the way there Robbie didn't say anything. It makes me really nervy when people don't speak. Dad says it's because I don't have much going on in my own head, which is hilarious coming from someone who knows all the words to "New York, New York".

When we got to the exact spot where we first kissed, Robbie looked at me. "Georgia, there isn't an easy way of saying this, but I'm going to have to go away."

I said, "Hahahahaha... I know, to Hamburger-a-gogo...

and I'm coming too. I've been practising saying 'Have a nice day', and I can very nearly say it without throwing up." I rambled on, but he stopped me.

"Georgia, love, I'm not going to Los Angeles. That interview I went to was for a placement on an ecological farm in New Zealand. And I've got it. I'm going to go live there for a year. It will be really, really hard to leave you, but I know it's the right thing to do."

"A placement... a... in... a... Kiwi-a-gogo... Maoris... sheep... the... it... I..."

In bed
Crying
A lot

How can this be happening to me? After all I've been through. The Sex God said he realised it was a shallow, hollow facsimile of a sham to be a popstar.

I said, "We could recycle our caviar tins."

But he was serious. I should have known when he turned up on his bike that something had gone horribly wrong.

1:30 p.m.

Kiwi-a-gogo land, though. Loads of sheep and bearded loons. And I am sure that the men would be just as bad.

Robbie flies off to Whakatane next week.

Next week.

Perhaps I am being paid back for having the Cosmic Horn.

1:35 p.m.

Robbie said maybe I could come over for a holiday when he was settled in. I cried and cried and tried to persuade him not to go, but he said this weird thing. He said, "Georgia, you know how much I like you, but you are only young, and I'm only young and we have to have some time to grow up before we settle down." And even though I was really really blubby, I felt a funny kind of reliefiosity.

4:00 p.m.

Phoned Jas and told her. She said "OhmyGod" about a million times. Then she came round and stayed overnight with me. She said I could wear her Ramblers' badge, but I said no, thank you.

In the middle of the night, in the dark, I said to her, "Jas, do you know what is weird?"

"What?"

"Well, you know I am on the brink of tragicosity and everything, but... well, I've got this sort of weird... weird..."

"What?"

"I'll tell you if you stop saying 'what'."

I could hear her chewing in the dark. What had she found to chew?

"I've got this weird feeling of reliefiosity."

And she said, "What, like when you need a poo and then you have a poo?"

Sunday February 6th

I've spoken to Robbie. He is upset, but he is definitely going.

He cried on the telephone.

5:30 p.m.

I am absolutely full of tragicosity. I went for a walk down to the square where the gang usually hangs out. I feel lonely as a clud.

Not lonely as a clud for long, because I bumped into Dave the Laugh, on his way to play snooker. He said, "Hello, groovster. How are you?"

I said, "A bit on the poo and *merde* side, to be honest."

"Yeah, me too. Do you fancy going down to the park and hanging out for a bit?"

He's really nice actually, almost normal, in fact, for a boy. He is upset that Ellen is upset, but he says it wouldn't be right to keep going out with her just because he felt sorry for her.

I said, "You are quite literally full of wisdomosity."

I told him about the Robbie fandango.

He smiled at me, "So then, Sex Queen, you are not going to go to Los Angeles, you are going to go to Whakatane and raise elks with Robbie?"

In my room
10:00 p.m.

Everyone is out. Mutti and Vati have gone out on a "date" and Libby is staying at her friend Josh's for the night.

Dave the Laugh and I talked for ages. About life and the universe and everything. Yes, we did. And then... we

SNOGGED again!!! I can't believe it!!! I am like Jekyll and Whatsit in babydoll pyjamas.

10:05 p.m.

I must have the Cosmic Horn because of spring (even though it is February).

Dave the Laugh said we are only teenagers and we haven't been teenagers before, so how can we know what we are supposed to do.

He's right, although I haven't a clue what he is talking about. He said we should just live live live for the moment!!! Blow our Cosmic Horn and be done with it.

I must do something. I feel like I am going to explode.

10:10 p.m.

Phoned Jas. "Jas."

"*Oui.*"

"Do you ever get the urge?"

"*Pardon?*"

"You know, to flow free and wild."

She was thinking. "Well, sometimes when Tom and I are alone in the house together."

"Yes..."

"We flick each other with flannels."

"Jas, you keep talking on the telephone and I will send out for help."

"It's good fun... what you do is..."

"Jas, Jas, guess what I am doing now."

"Are you dancing?"

"Yes, I am, my strange little pal. But what am I dancing in?"

"A bowl?"

"Jas, don't be silly. Concentrate. Try to get an image of me flowing wild and free."

"Are you dancing in... your PE knickers?"

"*Non*... I am DANCING IN MY NUDDY-PANTS!!!!"

And we both laughed like loons on loon tablets.

I danced for ages around the house in my nuddy-pants. Also, I did this brilliant thing – I danced in the front window just for a second while Mr Across the Road was drawing his curtains. He will never be sure if he saw a mirage or not.

That is the kind of person I am.

Not really the kind of person who goes and raises elks in Whakatane.

The end

Midnight

Looking out of my bedroom window (partially dressed).

I can see Angus, with a few of his sons and daughters, making an escape tunnel through Mr and Mrs Next Door's hedge. He's still blowing his horn, even though he has no horn to blow.

Surely God wouldn't have invented red bottomosity unless he was trying to tell me something. He is, as we all know, impotent. Or do I mean omnipotent? Anyway, He is some kind of potent. Perhaps He is saying, "Go forth, Georgia, and use your red bottom wisely."

That will be it. So I can snuggle down now, safe in the sanctity of my own unique bottomosity.

Hang on a minute, who is that? By the lamp post? Oh, it's Mark Big Gob with his latest girlfriend, walking home. He must have dumped the midget and moved on to bigger things, because this one at least reaches his waist. Still, I cannot point the finger of shame at him. None of us is perfect. Although I don't think it's entirely necessary for his mouth to be as big as it is. He is like part bloke, part blue whale.

1:00 a.m.
Still looking out the window.

Perhaps I could have Dave the Laugh as an unserious boyfriend, and for diplomatic world relations-type stuff, also have that gorgey French boy who gave me the rose in gay Paree.

Hmmm. Here come Mutti and Vati, back from their night out.

So, I could have the Cosmic Horn for now. And I could save the Sex God for later!!

Perfect. Providing he doesn't get a Kiwi accent and start snogging sheep.

So all's well that ends well in God's land.

I'll just say goodnight to the stars. Goodnight stars.

And the moon. Goodnight moon, you gorgeous, big, round, yellow, sexy thing.

Phew, I really have got the Cosmic Horn badly.

Mutti and Vati have got out of their car and although they are holding each other up, they are still not fighting, so all is still well with the world.

Hang on a minute. They're not holding each other up, they are snogging.

That is so sad. And disgusting.

The official and proper end.
Probably.

Georgia's Glossary

billio · From the Australian outback. A billycan was something Aborigines boiled their goodies up in, or whatever it is they eat. Anyway, billio means boiling things up. Therefore, "my cheeks ached like billio" means... er... very achy. I don't know why we say it. It's a mystery, like many things. But that's the beauty of life.

Boboland · As I have explained many, many times English is a lovely and exciting language full of sophisticosity. To go to sleep is "to go to bobos", so if you go to bed you are going to Boboland. It is an Elizabethan expression (oh, OK then, Libby made it up and she can be unreasonably violent if you don't join in with her).

Boxing Day · The day after Chrimboli Day (Christmas

Day – keep up). It is called Boxing Day because that is the day you are supposed to open your presents. You don't do it on Baby Jesus's birthday because that is when he is opening his presents (symbolically). How pleased he must have been to get some frankincense (not).

bum-oley · Quite literally bottom hole. I'm sorry, but you did ask. Say it proudly (with a cheery smile and a Spanish accent).

Changing of the Guards · Outside of Her Maj's pad (Buckingham Palace or Buck House as we call it) there are a load of blokes marching about with bearskins on their heads. They are guarding her against... er... stuff – the French, probably. After a bit they get tired and droopy and have to be changed for new ones.

Chrimbo/Chrimboli · Christmas Day, really, but as you know, time is money.

Churchill Square · A shopping centre (mall) named after Sir Winston Churchill who won World War II. (Although my grandad said *he* won the war by parachuting into Germany and landing on Hitler's motorbike and overcoming him with native cunning and superior military skills. What you have to take into consideration is that my grandad is bonkers.)

Cliff Richard's Y-Fronts · Y-Fronts are boys' knickers, but they are not worn by any boy you would want to know. Cliff Richard is a living legend (who is now a Lord – or is it a Lady?).

clud · This is short for cloud. Lots of really long boring poems and so on can be made much snappier by abbreviating words. So Wordsworth's poem called "Daffodils" (or "Daffs") has the immortal line "I wandered lonely as a clud." Ditto Rom and Jul. Or Ham. Or Merc of Ven.

conk · Nose. This is very interesting historically. A very long time ago (1066) – even before my grandad was born – a bloke called William the Conqueror (French) came to England and shot our King Harold in the eye. Typical. And people wonder why we don't like the French much. Anyway, William had a big nose and so to get our own back we called him William the Big Conkerer. If you see what I mean. I hope you do because I am exhausting myself with my hilariosity and historiosity.

David Beckham · Of course you know who David Beckham is. He is the sensationally vain English football captain. He is married to Posh Spice. But we love the little scallywag (don't start pretending you don't know what scallywag means).

DIY · Quite literally "Do It Yourself!" Rude when you think about it. Instead of getting someone competent to do things around the house (you know, like a trained electrician or a builder or a plumber), some vatis choose to do DIY. Always with disastrous results. (For example, my bedroom ceiling has footprints in it because my vati decided he would go up on the roof and replace a few tiles. Hopeless.)

duffing up · Duffing up is the female equivalent of beating up. It is not so violent and usually involves a lot of pushing with the occasional pinch.

duff · useless

Edith Piaf · Some French woman who used to sing "Je ne regrette rien", which means she didn't regret anything. Which is ironic as she was only four foot high and French.

first footing · Traditional Och Aye-land madness. On the stroke of midnight on December 31st some complete fool (a vati) knocks on your door and gives you a lump of coal. No one knows why. Ask the Scottish folk. And while you are at it, ask them about sporrans. And deep fried pizza.

first former · Kids of about eleven who have just started "big" school. They have shiny innocent faces, very tempting to slap.

fringe · Goofy short bit of hair that comes down to your eyebrows. Someone told me that American-type people call them "bangs" but this is so ridiculously strange that it's not worth thinking about. Some people can look very stylish with a fringe (i.e., me) while others look goofy (Jas). The Beatles started it apparently. One of them had a German girlfriend, and she cut their hair with a pudding bowl, and the rest is history.

geoggers · Geoggers is short for geography. Ditto

blodge (biology) and lunck (lunch).

gusset · Do you really not know what a gusset is? I do.

horn · When you "have the horn" it's the same as "having the big red bottom".

Isle of Man · A ridiculous Island in the sea in between Scotland and Ireland. You travel on a boat full of mad people being tossed about like a cork. Then you get there and it's full of people from Liverpool, and the most exciting thing about it is that the cats don't have tails. Honestly.

Kiwi-a-gogo land · New Zealand. "A-gogo land" can be used to liven up the otherwise really boring names of other countries. America, for instance, is Hamburger-a-gogo land. Mexico is Mariachi-a-gogo land and France is Frogs'-legs-a-gogo land.

Michael Parkinson · He interviews people on a TV chat show. He has very nice grey hair and shiny suits. Like a badger. But without the big digging paws. As far as I know.

nippy noodles · Instead of saying "Good heavens, it's quite cold this morning" you say "Cor – nippy noodles!!" English is an exciting and growing language. It is. Believe me. Just leave it at that. Accept it.

nub · The heart of the matter. You can also say gist and thrust. This is from the name for the centre of a wheel where the spokes come out. Or do I mean hub? Who cares. I feel a dance coming on.

nuddy-pants · Quite literally nude-coloured pants, and you know what nude-coloured pants are? They are no pants. So if you are in your nuddy-pants you are in your no pants, i.e., you are naked.

nunga-nungas · Basoomas. Girls' breasty business. Ellen's brother calls them nunga-nungas because he says that if you get hold of a girl's breast and pull it out and then let it go – it goes nunga-nunga-nunga. As I have said many, many times with great wisdomosity, there is something really wrong with boys.

Old Bill · The police, a.k.a. "the filth" or "our brave lads in blue". Depending on whether they can hear you or not.

piggies · Pigtails. Or bunches. Like two little side ponytails in your hair. Only we think they look like pigtails. English people are obsessed with pigs; that is our strange beauty.

porkies · Amusing(ish) Cockney rhyming slang. Pork pies = lies. Which is of course shortened to porkies. Oh, that isn't shorter, is it? Well, you can't have everything.

prat · A prat is a gormless oik. You make a prat of yourself by mistakenly putting both legs down one knicker leg or by playing air guitar at pop concerts.

rate · To fancy someone. Like I fancy (or rate) the Sex God. And I certainly do fancy the SG as anyone with the brains of an earwig (i.e., not Jas) would know by now. Phew – even writing about him in the glossary has made me go all jelloid. And stupidoid.

Rolf Harris · An Australian "entertainer" (not). Rolf has a huge beard and glasses. He plays the didgeridoo, which says everything in my book. He sadly has had a number of hit records, which means he is never off TV and will not go back to Australia. (His "records" are called "Tie Me Kangaroo Down, Sport", etc.)

spondulicks · A Sudanese term for money. Possibly. The reason we use it is because in olden days English people used to go to other countries where the weather was nicer (i.e., everywhere) and say to the leaders of these other countries, "Hello, what extremely nice weather you are having, do you like our flag?" And the other (not English) people would say, "Yes, it's very nice, is it a Union Jack?" And the old English people would reply, "Yes. Where is your flag?" And they would say, "We haven't got one actually." And we'd say, "Oh dear. That means you have to give your country to us then." That is how we became world leaders and also how we got foreign words in our language. By the way, it's a very good job that I have historiosity at my fingertips, otherwise certain people (i.e., you) would feel hopelessly dim.

Sporrans · Ah, I'm glad you asked me about this because it lets me illustrate my huge knowledgosity about Och Aye land. Sporrans are bits of old sheep that Scotsmen wear over their kilts, at the front, like little

furry aprons. Please don't ask me why; I feel a nervy spaz
coming on.

P.S.
Turn the page for a peek at
my next book...

'...and that's when it fell off in my hand.'

Further fabbitty-fab confessions of Georgia Nicolson

Louise Rennison

www.georgianicolson.com

Alone, all aloney, on my owney

Saturday March 5th
11:00 a.m. as the crow flies

Grey skies, grey cluds, grey knickers.

I can't believe my knickers are grey, but it is typico of my life. My mutti put my white lacy knickers in the wash with Vati's voluminous black shorts and now they are grey.

If there was a medal for craposity in the mutti department, she would win it hands down.

I am once again wandering lonely as a clud through this Vale of Tears.

I wish there was someone I could duff up but I have no one to blame. Except God, and although He is everywhere at once, He is also invisible. (Also, the last person who tried to duff God up was Satan, and he ended up standing on his head in poo with hot swords up his bum-oley.)

11:20 a.m.

This is my fabulous life: the Sex God left for Whakatane last month and he has taken my heart with him.

11:25 a.m.

Not literally, of course, otherwise there would be a big hole in my nunga-nungas.

11:28 a.m.

And also I would be dead. Which quite frankly would be a blessing in disguise.

12:00 p.m.

It is soooo boring being brokenhearted. My eyes look like little piggie eyes from crying. Which makes my nose look ginormous.

Still, at least I am a lurker-free zone. Although with my luck there will be a lurker explosion any minute.

Alison Bummer once had a double yolker on her neck; she had a big spot and it had a baby spot growing on top of it.

I'll probably get that.

12:05 p.m.

Phoned my very bestest pally, Jas.

"Jas, it's me."

"What?"

"Jas, you don't sound very pleased to hear from me."

"Well... I would be, but it's only five minutes since you last phoned and Tom is just telling me about this thing you can do. You go off into the forest and—"

"This hasn't got anything to do with badgers, has it?"

"Well... no, not exactly, it's a wilderness course and you learn how to make fire and so on."

Oh great balls of *merde* here we go, off into the land of the terminally insane, i.e. Jasland. I said as patiently as I could because I am usually nice(ish) to the disadvantaged, "You are going off on a course to learn how to make fire?"

"Yes, exciting, eh?"

"Why do you have to go on a course to learn how to open a box of matches?"

"You can't use matches."

"Why not?"

"Because it's a wilderness course."

"No, wrong, Jas, it's a crap course where people are too mean to give you any matches."

She did that sighing business.

"Look, Georgia, I know you're upset about Robbie going off to Kiwi-a-gogo land."

"I am."

"And you not having a boyfriend or anything."

"Yes, well..."

"And, you know, being all lonely, with no one to really care about you."

"Yes, all right Jas, I know all th—"

"And the days stretching ahead of you without any meaning and—"

"Jas, shut up."

"I'm only trying to say that—"

"That is not shutting up, Jas. It is going on and on."

She got all huffy and Jasish.

"I must go now. Tom has got some knots to show me."

I was in the middle of saying, "Yes I bet he has..." in an ironic and *très amusant* way when she brutally put the phone down.

12:30 p.m.

Alone, all aloney.

On my owney.

The house is empty, too. Everyone is out at Grandad's for lunch.

I was nearly made to go until I pointed out that I am in mourning and unable to eat anything because of my heartbreak.

Mine is a pathetico tale that would make anyone who had a heart weep, but that does not include Vati. He said he would gladly leave me behind because talking to me made him realise the fun he had had when he accidentally fell into the open sewers in India.

1:15 p.m.

Looking out of my bedroom window. Entombed in my room for ever. Like in that book, *The Prisoner of Brenda,* or whatever it's called.

Except I could go out if I wanted.

But I don't want to.

I may never go out again.

Ever.

1:30 p.m.

This is boring. I've been cooped up for about a million years.

What time is it?

Phoned Jas.

"Jas?"

"Oh God."

"What time is it?"

"What?"

"Why are you saying 'what'? I merely asked you a civil question."

"Why don't you look at your own clock?"

"Jas, have you noticed I am very, very upset and that my life is over? Have you noticed that?"

"Yes I have, because you have been on the phone telling me every five minutes for a month."

"Well, I am soo sorry if it's too much trouble to tell your very bestest pal the time. Perhaps my eyes are too swollen from tears to see the clock."

"Well are they?"

"Yes."

"Well how come you could see to dial my number?"

Mrs Huffy Knickers was so unreasonable.

"Anyway, I'm not your bestest pal any more, Nauseating P. Green is your bestest pal now that you rescued her from the clutches of the Bummer twins."

I slammed down the phone.

Brilliant. Sex Godless and now friend to P. Green, that well-known human goldfish.

Sacré bloody *bleu* and triple *merde*.

And poo.

Oh Robbie, how could you leave me and go off to the other (incredibly crap) side of the world? What has Kiwi-a-gogo land got that I haven't? Besides forty million sheep.

I think I'll play the tape he gave me again. It's all I have left to remind me of him and our love. That will never die.

2:20 p.m.

Good grief, now I am really depressed. His song about Van Gogh, "Oh No, It's Me Again", has to be one of the most depressing songs ever written.

2:30 p.m.

Second only to track four, "Swim Free", about a dolphin that gets caught in a fishing net, and every time we eat a tuna sandwich we're eating Sammy the dolphin. Fortunately I never eat tuna, as Mum mostly stocks up on Jammy Dodgers and there is definitely nothing that was ever alive in them.

2:35 p.m.

If I am brutally honest, which I try to be, the only fly in the ointmosity of the Sex God was that he could be a bit on the serious side. Always raving on about the environment and so on. Actually, his whole family is obsessed with vegetables. Let's face it, his brother Tom (otherwise known as Hunky) has chosen one to be his girlfriend!

Hahahahahaha. That's a really good joke about Jas that I will never tell her but secretly think of when she flicks her fringe about or shows me her Rambler's badge.

I will never forget Robbie, though. The way he used to nibble my lips. He will always be Nip Libbler Extraordinaire.

2:50 p.m.

Oh no, hang on. The Sex God used to snog my ears. It was Dave the Laugh who enticed me into the ways of nip libbling. Which reminds me. I wonder why he hasn't phoned me?

Did I remember to tell him that I was thinking about letting him be my unserious boyfriend?

I should punish him, really. It was, after all, he who introduced me to the Cosmic Horn when I was happy just having the Particular Horn for the Sex God.

2:55 p.m.
Phoned Rosie.

"RoRo."

"*Bonsoir.*"

"I am having the cosmic droop."

"Well, fear not, my pally, because I have *le* plan *de la* genius."

"What is it, and does it involve the police?"

Rosie laughed in a not-very-reassuring way if you like the sound of sane laughter. She said, "I'm having a party for Sven's return from Swedenland next Saturday."

"What kind of party is it going to be?"

"Teenage werewolf."

"Oh no."

"Oh yes."

"Good grief."

"Bless you."

"Rosie, what has Sven been doing while he's been away, working for Santa Claus on a reindeer farm?"

"He hasn't been to Lapland."

"How can you be sure? Geoggers is not your best subject, is it?"

"Well, excuse me if I'm right, but it isn't yours either, Gee. You missed out the whole of Germany on your world map."

"Easily done."

"Not when you're copying from the atlas. Anyway, I must go. I have a costume to make. See you at Stalag 14 on Monday."

Bathroom

3:00 p.m.

Sometimes I amaze myself with my courageosity. Even though I have been through the mangle of love and beyond, I can still be bothered to cleanse and tone.

3:30 p.m.

But the effort of a high-quality beauty regime has made me exhausted. I am going to go to my room and read my book on my inner dolphin or whatever it's called. Anyway it is to do with peace and so on. I may even make a little shrine to Robbie to celebrate our undying love. Even though he hasn't bothered to write to me since he went to Kiwi-a-gogo land.

3:45 p.m.

Hmm. I have covered all the cosmic options with my shrine: I've put a photo of Robbie in the middle of some shiny paper, it has a figure of Buddha on one side of the beloved Sex God, and one of Jesus and a little dish for offerings on the other. Also, when I was accidentally going through Mum's knicker drawer, I found some incense stuff. I don't like to think what she and Vati do with it: some horrific snogging ritual they learned in Katmandu or something.

3:50 p.m.

I had to BluTack Jesus on to my dressing table because Libby has been using him as a boyfriend for scuba-diving Barbie and one of his feet is missing.

4:00 p.m.
Phoned Rosie.

"RoRo, explain this if you can with your wisdomosity. I only had the Particular Horn for SG before I met Dave the Laugh and then Dave the Laugh lured me into the web of the General and Cosmic Horns."

RoRo said, "He's groovy, isn't he, Dave the Laugh?"

"Yeah... sort of."

"Shall I ask him on Saturday?"

"It doesn't matter to me, because I am eschewing him with a firm hand."

"A nod is as good as a wink to a blind badger."

What in the name of Miss Wilson's moustache is she talking about?

Sunday March 6th

Dreamed about the Sex God and our marriage. It was really groovy and gorgey. I wore a long white veil, and when I was at the altar SG pushed it back and said, "Why... Georgia, you're beautiful." And I didn't go cross-eyed or speak in a stupid German accent. I even remembered to put my tongue at the back of my teeth to stop my nostrils flaring when I smiled. The church was packed with loads of friends, and everyone looked nice and relatively normal. Even Vati had shaved the tiny badger off his chin, and Uncle Eddie had a hat on so that he didn't look quite so much like a boiled egg in a suit.

The choir was singing "Isn't She Lovely?" and for some reason the choir was made up of chipmunks and Libby was in charge of them. It was sweet, even if the singing was a bit high-pitched.

And then the vicar said, "Is there anyone here who knows of any reason why these two should not be joined in matrimony?"

I was gazing into the dark blue of Sex God's eyes, dreamy dreamy. Then from the back, Jackie Bummer (smoking a fag) shouted, "I've got a reason: Georgia has got extreme red-bottomosity."

And Alison Bummer (smoking two fags) joined in, "Yeah, and the Cosmic Horn."

And I could feel myself getting hotter and hotter, and I couldn't breathe. I woke up crying out to find Libby sitting on my nungas with Charlie Horse and singing, "Smelly the elepan bagged her trunk and said goodguy to the circus."